Emma Dilemma and the Camping Nanny

by Patricia Hermes

Marshall Cavendish Children

For Logan, Madeline, and McClain Hermes

Marshall Cavendish Corporation
99 White Plains Road
Tarrytown, NY 10591
www.marshallcavendish.us/kids

Library of Congress Cataloging-in-Publication Data
Hermes, Patricia.
Emma Dilemma and the camping nanny/ Patricia Hermes.—1st ed.
p. cm.
Summary: Nine-year-old Emma O'Fallon finds herself in increasing difficulties as
her complicated efforts to break up the growing attachment between Annie, the
Irish nanny, and Bo, her boyfriend, cause chaos on a family camping trip and her
own relationship with her best friend Luisa seems to be going from bad to worse.
ISBN 978-0-7614-5534-9
[1. Friendship—Fiction. 2. Jealousy—Fiction. 3. Nannies—Fiction.
4. Camping—Fiction. 5. Conduct of life—Fiction. 6. Family life—Fiction.]
I. Title.
PZ7.H4317Emc 2009
[Fic]—dc22
2008038809

Book design by Virginia Pope
Editor: Margery Cuyler
Printed in China
First edition
1 3 5 6 4 2

m͡c Marshall Cavendish
Children

Other **Emma Dilemma** Books

Emma Dilemma and the New Nanny
Emma Dilemma and the Two Nannies
Emma Dilemma and the Soccer Nanny

Dad

McClain

Annie

Emma

Lizzie + Ira

Tim

Mom

Contents

Chapter One
A Big Stupid Dilemma

"*Stupid!*" Emma said. "*Stupid, stupid, stupid!*" She was kneeling on the window seat in her room, peering out the window.

"Stupid!" she muttered again.

Stupid was a word she wasn't allowed to say. Nobody in the house was allowed to say it. And *hate*, too, was another one. Those words got you in trouble. *Stupid* was the first word the twins, Ira and Lizzie, had learned to say when they started talking. They had learned it from Emma. Now nobody was allowed to say it.

But the twins weren't in Emma's room, and neither were McClain, Emma's five-year-old sister, and Tim, Emma's big brother and best friend. Mom and Daddy weren't around either so Emma said it again, out loud.

"Annie's acting stupid! And Bo is really, really

stupid. Even his name is stupid. His car is stupid, too. I hate him hanging around."

Emma leaned closer to the window to see better. Bo's little red car with the dumb plastic daisy on the antenna was parked in the driveway. It was dark out, and Annie had turned on the floodlights in the driveway by the basketball hoop. She and Bo were playing "horse." Woof, the family's huge, fluffy poodle, was barking, jumping up and down, and running after the ball.

Emma was supposed to be asleep. Earlier, Daddy had let her borrow his laptop computer because her computer didn't work for movies. She had planned on watching *The Wizard of Oz*, her absolute favorite. Daddy said she could if she promised to go to sleep as soon as the movie ended. But how could she sleep?

Annie was their nanny. She came from Ireland, and she talked funny and wore weird kinds of clothes, and she was the best nanny in the whole wide world. Emma knew a lot about nannies! There had been a bunch of really horrible ones before Annie arrived. Annie had been with them only a few months, but already Emma loved her more than just about anyone. Annie had her own apartment on the third floor of their house. She took care of the kids and loved them and played with them and everything! A couple of times, she even got in trouble when they did, because she sometimes acted like a kid herself. But Emma knew her parents loved Annie almost as much as the kids did. Mom and Daddy even said that Annie was family.

Except now Annie had a stupid boyfriend. And she didn't spend nearly as much of her free time with Emma's family as she used to. And suppose she . . . well, Emma couldn't even think about that.

She leaned closer to the window, moving the laptop carefully aside. Annie and stupid Bo must have moved nearer to the house, because Emma couldn't see them anymore. But she could hear Annie laughing. Emma thought of opening the window, but she didn't want Annie to know she was spying.

She listened some more. Annie's voice floated up, though Emma couldn't hear what she was saying. Annie must have been standing right beneath Emma's window.

There has to be a way to see her down there, Emma thought. Maybe if she were a little taller, she could see better? She grabbed some books that were on the window seat, piled them up, and slowly climbed on top of them.

She stood on tiptoe, leaning against the window.

Yes, she could just see the top of Annie's head. Was she holding hands with Bo?

Emma pressed her nose against the glass.

The books began to slide. They slipped sideways. Emma could feel them tumbling out from beneath her. Help! She tilted this way. That. She tried to catch herself. But she fell. Backward off the seat and onto the floor, books and seat cushion scattered around her. She landed on her bottom. But her arm! As she fell, she scraped it along the wooden roof of her dollhouse beside the window seat. It hurt!

She looked down. Her arm was scratched and kind of bloody. Not only that, but as she fell, the laptop fell with her. It lay beside her on the floor with the top popped open. Tears sprang to Emma's eyes. She started to yell out, "Mom! Daddy! Annie!"

But she clamped her mouth shut.

Stupid!

She picked up the laptop. She shut the top, then turned the laptop 'round and 'round and looked at it carefully. It didn't seem to be hurt. There were no wires sticking out or anything. Phew.

She lay it down on the rug and looked at her arm. It was badly scratched. She wished her arm were broken. Then Annie would have to spend lots of time with her and not with Bo. But no, she didn't want it broken, not really. She couldn't play soccer with her arm in a cast. Soccer season was over, and her team had actually won the championship, but she still had to go to practice for next spring—though half the team had dropped out. Even Emma's best friend, Luisa, kept making excuses for getting out of practice. Luisa and mean Katie were busy with some hip-hop dance thing, getting ready for a concert. Emma hardly ever saw Luisa anymore. Also, Emma had found out that Luisa and Katie sent instant messages to each other almost every day.

Emma knew what would make her feel better. Marmaduke and Marshmallow, her pet ferrets, the sweetest, cuddliest ferrets in the whole world. She got a tissue from her nightstand and wiped her bloody scrape, then went over to their cage.

Marshmallow was asleep. But Marmaduke was awake. He was looking up at Emma, his eyes round and wide. Emma thought he seemed worried. He had probably heard her fall.

"Want to come in bed with me?" she whispered.

Marmaduke nodded.

Emma unlatched the cage and lifted him out. She closed the cage top and locked it. It was hard to do with just one hand, but if the latch wasn't closed right, Marshmallow might get out. Emma brought Marmaduke over to her bed and crawled with him beneath the covers.

Marmaduke snuggled under Emma's chin. He snuffled at her. Marmaduke always seemed to understand when Emma was worried or upset. He made himself extra-snuggly at those times, tucking himself tight against her body.

"Marmaduke," Emma whispered. "What am I going to do about Annie? I know she's supposed to be with us only during the week—daytimes. Nights and weekends she's free. Except lots of times she plays with us, even if it is her time off. At least, she used to! Now she's always with stupid Bo. And she wears his stupid bracelet. She doesn't even have Sunday night supper with us anymore."

Marmaduke snuffled again. He understood.

Emma pretended that Marmaduke really did know what she was saying and was talking back to her. She gave Marmaduke a little baby voice.

"I know," she made Marmaduke whisper in his baby-type voice. "She *likes* to be with you. Used to like to be with you. Even in her free time. Now it's just Bo, Bo, Bo!"

"Right!" Emma said back in her own voice. "It's like I don't even count anymore. Annie's gotten as bad as Luisa—busy, busy, busy! No time for us. For me."

Marmaduke sighed. He didn't have anything more to say. He totally understood. He snuggled closer under Emma's chin.

Marmaduke loved Annie, too. Emma was sure of that. And Annie loved him back, not like some nannies who hated ferrets. One of the nannies before Annie had even tried to kill Marmaduke with a broom when she saw him running around the house. She thought he was a rat.

Annie would never do anything like that. But why didn't Annie know how much Emma missed her? And how worried she was?

It was just too, too stupid. Emma had to do something about it. "You got to help me, buddy," she whispered to Marmaduke. "I need a plan."

But Marmaduke was sound asleep. And Emma was wide, wide awake. And hurting.

Chapter Two
Tim Helps

Emma didn't know how long she lay awake. She just knew it was a long, long time. After a while, she couldn't stand it anymore. Her arm hurt, and she was worried about Annie and Bo. She needed a plan, and she knew just who could help her.

Carefully, she lifted the sleeping Marmaduke, put him back in his cage, and locked the top. Then she slid her feet into her frog slippers. She loved her frog slippers because the frogs seemed as if they could talk to her, too, just like Marmaduke. Sometimes they looked very solemn, as if they were nodding at her, agreeing with her. Other times, when she wiggled her toes, they even winked at her.

Tonight, they just looked asleep.

She opened her door, peeked into the hall, and

listened. The whole house was quiet and asleep. There was no light coming from underneath anyone's door, not even Mom and Daddy's. Woof lay at the end of the hall by the door to Annie's upstairs apartment. He looked up, wagged his little stubby tail, and put his head back down again.

Emma tiptoed along the hall, past the twins' room, past McClain's room, past Mom and Daddy's room. Quietly, she opened the door to Tim's room and tiptoed over to his bed. "Tim?" she whispered. "Wake up!"

She stared down at him. Well, what she could see of him. He had the covers pulled tight over his head. He always slept that way. He was ten years old, only ten and a half months older than she was. He said he was too old to believe in nighttime monsters. But Emma had a feeling that maybe he wasn't exactly sure. Still, he was a great older brother, the best in the world.

And now, Emma needed him. Even though it was just after midnight. She could see the clock on his bedside table blinking off the seconds.

"Tim?" she whispered again, a little louder.

Tim sat straight up. "What?" he said. "Is it time for school? I'm late!" He pushed back the covers and threw his legs over the side of the bed.

"No!" Emma whispered. "It's not school time.

It's midnight. Get back in bed. I just want to tell you something."

Tim pulled his legs in and flopped back on his pillow. "You always do this!" he grumbled.

"I do not," Emma said. Though she did. Sometimes.

"What's the matter now?" Tim said, still grumpy sounding.

"I'm scared."

Tim sat up again. With the light from his computer screen, Emma could see that Tim's eyes were wide open and surprised looking. "*You?*" he said. "*You* scared? You're never scared."

Emma smiled. She liked him saying that. And it was kind of true. She didn't get scared about much, except for doctors and shots and sometimes other little stuff.

"Well, I'm scared now," Emma said. "I mean, worried."

Tim reached over and turned on his bedside lamp. The light made Emma blink. "Did Marmaduke get out again?" Tim asked. "Or Marshmallow?"

"Nope," Emma said, shaking her head. She smiled, though, thinking about how many times Marmaduke had escaped. And then Woof would chase him, and sometimes Kelley, the cat, got into the act, and everything became a big madhouse.

"It's not that," Emma said, sinking down on Tim's bed. "Tim, I'm worried. And look. My arm. I hurt it."

She pushed up the sleeve of her pajamas and showed him the scrape.

Tim made a face. "Yuck! Does it hurt lots?"

"Not too much," Emma said. And then she remembered that Tim sometimes got a little scared of blood, so she pulled her sleeve back down.

"How'd you do that? When?"

"Just before. I fell off the window seat," Emma said. "I was standing up on a pile of books, looking out the window, and I slipped. I put my hand out to save myself and scraped my arm on the dollhouse."

"You want me to wake up Mom? I'll go get her," Tim said.

"No!" Emma said. "It's not that bad."

Tim frowned. "How could you fall so hard? I mean, off the window seat?"

Emma sighed. "Because I was trying to see out the window better, and I couldn't see enough from the window seat, so I thought if I were up higher, I could see better because they were standing kind of close to the house. But then the books slipped and . . ."

"Who was close to the house?" Tim said.

"Annie! And Bo!" She said *Bo* as if it were a bad word, as if it smelled.

Tim sighed.

"He's her *boyfriend!*" Emma said. She said that word, too, like it smelled.

"He's not a boyfriend. She told us that."

"Then what is he?"

"He's just a friend who happens to be a boy!" Tim said. "Remember how she said that? She told us that she wasn't going to get married and leave us, and that—"

"See, you're worried about it, too!" Emma interrupted.

"Am not," Tim said. "I'm just saying. She said she wouldn't get married, not till we are all grown up, not till Ira and Lizzie are grown up, and they're still just three, and McClain is only five, so we have lots of time."

It was a long speech for Tim. He was kind of quiet, usually. But the way he blurted it out like that told Emma he was worried about Annie and Bo as much as she was.

"Yeah, well," Emma said, "she told us that before she met Bo. Before he gave her that bracelet."

"Doesn't matter," Tim said. And then he frowned. "Were they like . . . kissing?"

Emma shook her head. "No. But they were

12

laughing a lot. And maybe holding hands. I think."

Tim scrunched up his face.

"And Tim," Emma went on. "Know how Annie sometimes has supper with us on Friday and Sunday nights? Or she used to? But she doesn't anymore. Not even Sundays when we have pizza. And you know how she loves pizza!"

"Yeah. I know."

"That's because we don't count anymore. She's always with *him*."

"No," Tim said. "It's 'cause Sunday is her Irish dance thing. Remember how we went to watch her that night and how weird they dance, like robots? They don't move their arms or anything."

"Yeah," Emma said. "I remember. Robot puppets. But are you sure it was Sunday? I thought it was Saturday."

"I'm sure," Tim said. "Because remember? When we went, McClain wanted to change out of her church dress and put on her bathing suit and Mom said no, she had to wear her church dress and McClain had a big fit."

Emma nodded. She did remember. Not that it was anything surprising. McClain was always having big fits. She also hated clothes and wore her bathing suit every chance she got, even now that it was almost winter.

13

"So that's how I know," Tim said. "And that's where she goes Sunday nights."

"Yeah, but Bo goes, too, right?" Emma said.

Tim nodded.

"See?" Emma said. "That's what I said. She's always with him."

"Yeah," Tim said. "I guess. But maybe that's just because Bo likes to dance."

Emma was quiet for a minute. And suddenly, a thought began to grow inside her head. An idea. A good idea! Maybe even a great idea. She had known Tim would help her. Even if he didn't know that he had helped.

Emma looked down at her frog slippers. She wiggled her toes. The frogs were awake now. They winked at her.

Emma smiled.

"Okay, Tim," Emma said, standing up. "You can go back to sleep now. Thanks. Sorry I woke you up."

"Okay. But . . . I mean, thanks for what?"

"Because that was a great idea."

"It was? What was it?" Tim said.

"Never mind," Emma said.

She didn't think she wanted to spell it out for Tim just yet. She needed to think about it some more. But she had a wonderful idea, a plan, one that might be the very thing to take care of this really big dilemma. She might be able to solve it, very, very soon.

Chapter Three

Emma Has a Better Plan

The next morning, Emma scurried down the hall to Tim's room. She had put on a long-sleeved shirt so Mom and Daddy wouldn't see her scrape and ask how it happened.

She was ready to tell Tim her plan. She had stayed up almost all night thinking about it.

The only thing was, Tim wasn't in his room to hear it. She could hear him downstairs talking, could hear the whole family bubbling around in the dining room.

Rats. Emma needed Tim—alone. Tim always thought a lot about plans and about what Mom called consequences. And Emma sometimes didn't. Like the time she got all her brothers and sisters to go on strike, but then a newspaper lady learned about it and wrote a story in the newspaper—the front page of the local paper! That was "bad consequences." Mom got so mad that time she could hardly speak. Things worked out all right in the end, though, and nobody got in trouble. Not too much trouble, anyway.

Emma was about to race downstairs for breakfast, when she remembered something. She went back to her room. She had to set Marmaduke and Marshmallow free from their cage for a while. She did that every morning before school and at night, too. Emma knew that ferrets needed lots of time to run free, and as long as Emma made sure that they were closed up in her room, Mom didn't mind if they ran around. Emma just had to remember to put them back in their cage before she left for school and clean up any mess they might make.

She lifted Marmaduke gently, kissed the top of his head, and set him down on the floor. Next, she picked up Marshmallow and kissed her, too. Marshmallow snuggled under Emma's chin for a minute.

"Good girl!" Emma whispered. "Did Marmaduke teach you that?"

Marshmallow just snuffled. Marshmallow was Emma's newest ferret and hadn't yet learned all the tricks, like snuggling and nodding back when Emma spoke to her, the way Marmaduke did. But Marshmallow was learning quickly.

When they were both free, Emma went out and closed the door tightly behind her. She ran downstairs, excited that Daddy was home. Daddy was a pilot, and some weeks he was on a trip, flying his plane to Ireland. When he was gone, Emma missed him a lot. But he had come back home yesterday, and last night at dinner, he said that today the family could plan something together. School was going to be closed tomorrow, Friday, for teacher workshops, so they'd have a three-day weekend to go somewhere. Mom worked some days at the museum in the city, but she said she could take Friday off, too.

Emma wished they could go to Disney World, but she knew they couldn't, not for just three days. Anyway, they'd gone there last year, and the trip was a big mess. When the twins saw Mickey Mouse walking down the street, they chased after him and disappeared into the crowd. McClain somehow got into the tree house by herself when nobody was looking. Even though all three kids got found in like three minutes, Mom and Daddy said those three minutes were crazy-terrifying. Mom said, "That's it, never again."

Now, when Emma got to the dining room, everybody was already seated around the table. Tim was sitting beside Daddy, with one of Daddy's big books about the sky and constellations spread out in front of him. McClain was wearing a mad face and had her arms folded over her chest—as if that were anything new. Mom was at the end of the table reading the paper. And the toddler twins, Ira and Lizzie, were bouncing around in their booster chairs like little helium balloons.

"Good morning, sleepyhead," Mom said, looking up from the newspaper and smiling. "You slept late. You're usually the first one down. You didn't stay up watching that movie, did you?"

Emma shook her head. "No," she said. "I didn't." She had stayed up late. But she didn't think Mom needed to know *why*.

"Emma!" Lizzie cried out, bopping up and down in her chair. "Guess what, guess what? We're going cramping."

"Not cramping, camping!" Ira said.

"That's what I said!" Lizzie said.

"Are we? Really?" Emma said, turning to Daddy and smiling. She loved camping with the family, especially times like now when it was getting cold and they made campfires and roasted marshmallows and sang songs and stuff. "When?"

"Tomorrow. And Saturday, too!" Tim answered, looking up from his book. "It's a full moon. And it's a blue moon, right, Dad?"

"Right," Daddy said.

"What's that?" Emma asked.

"It's when there are two full moons in one month," Tim answered.

"But they won't let me take Kelley!" McClain said, her face still pulled into a dark frown. She looked like one of those video game characters who swells up right before exploding.

Kelley was McClain's cat, and McClain took her just about everywhere, slinging her around as if she were a stuffed animal. Sometimes McClain even dressed Kelley in doll clothes, and Kelley didn't scratch or anything.

"You can't take cats," Ira said. "Because of—"

"Because cats run away and get lost in the woods," Lizzie said.

"Because the woods are dark," Ira said. "And . . . ."

"And, and scary!" Lizzie said.

"But not that scary," Ira said.

Lately the twins had taken to finishing one another's sentences, as if they were one person split into two little bodies.

"Enough, you two!" Mom said. "And you, too, McClain. Stop carrying on. You know very well you can't take a cat camping."

"You said we're taking Woof!" McClain said.

20

"That's different," Daddy said. "Woof's a dog." He grinned at Emma and wiggled his fingers, his signal that she should go to him. "Come over here! I haven't had enough hugs since I got back."

Emma went and stood beside his chair, leaning against him. He wrapped one arm around her waist and smiled up at her.

"So we're really going?" she asked.

"We are," Daddy said. "If everyone wants to."

And then Emma had a thought. "Can I bring a friend?" she asked.

Daddy looked at Mom. Mom looked at Daddy. They both shrugged.

"Sure, why not?" Daddy said.

Emma smiled. "Oh, thanks!" she said. She'd ask Luisa. She could have Luisa all to herself for the weekend. No Katie. Just her and Luisa together.

"I'll bring *Lizzie*," Ira said.

"I'll bring *you*," Lizzie said.

"Not me!" McClain said. "I'm not going without Kelley."

Emma turned to Mom. Mom hadn't said anything. Emma knew Mom didn't like camping all that much. Mom always said her idea of camping was staying at a Holiday Inn. But Mom was smiling. "Sure," she said. "It will be fun. Especially since Annie's coming along to help out."

21

"Annie's coming!" Emma said. "Yippee!" And then she frowned. "But it's a weekend."

"Yes, I know," Mom said. "But we all talked about it last night when Annie came in, and we invited her along, and she agreed to come. She said she'd never been camping before."

Emma smiled. She sent a look to Tim. He smiled back. Annie *did* love them. Loved being with them. Even on her days off.

"We agreed to trade off days," Daddy said. "She asked if she could take Tuesday off, since I'm going to be home all next week."

Mom smiled across the table at Daddy. "Annie sounded very excited about that."

Emma made a face. "She did? About what?" she asked.

"Something with Irish dance," Mom said.

"I thought that was Sunday nights," Emma said, looking at Tim.

"It is," Mom said. "But this is something else—a dance contest of some kind."

"Right," Daddy said. "It's a whole weeklong contest. Every day a different group competes. Annie's day is Tuesday. They were both very excited about it."

"*Both?*" Emma said. "Who?"

"Annie and Bo," Daddy said. "So I'm glad we

can give Annie the day off."

"What do you mean, Annie and *Bo*?" Emma said. She said it louder than she had meant to. Kind of mean-sounding, too.

Daddy tilted his head and raised his eyebrows. Mom put down the paper and frowned at her.

"I mean," Emma said, "I just meant . . ."

And then—well, she knew she should wait to ask Tim about "consequences." But she couldn't wait.

"I just meant I want to do Irish dance, too," she said. "And I can't if it's daytimes. I have school."

Tim popped his head up from his book. He stared at her, wide-eyed.

Daddy just laughed. "No way, sweet pea. You have enough activities, especially with soccer practices. You don't need to add dancing to your schedule. Besides, Annie needs some time without kids." He pulled Emma closer and hugged her tight against him.

"Ow!" she cried. She pulled away. She held her hurt arm against her side.

"What?" Daddy said. He reached out, but she backed farther away. "Honey, I'm sorry! What is it? Did I hurt you?"

Emma shook her head. "No! It's . . . it's nothing. It . . . it just hurts a little bit."

"What hurts?" Daddy said.

She couldn't tell! They'd ask how she did it. They'd know she was spying on Annie.

"It's nothing!" Emma said. "You just shouldn't squeeze so hard!" She made a mad face at him, then slid into a chair across from Tim.

Tim raised his eyebrows and sent her a look, a question. Emma knew just what he was asking—*How bad is it?*

Plenty bad, Emma told him with her eyes.

But not as bad as Annie going off for a whole day with Bo. Now what? What could Emma possibly do to make Bo disappear?

Chapter Four
Best Friends Trouble

Well, maybe she couldn't make Bo disappear. But she sure could get in his way. She had seen enough TV shows to know that grown-ups didn't like little kids hanging around when they had boyfriends or girlfriends. So Emma's plan—the one she had dreamed up when she'd been awake half the night—was to be a pest, to hang around Annie and Bo constantly. She'd be so annoying, such a big, fat nuisance, that Bo would surely give up. And part one of that plan was to figure out a way to go to Irish dance on Sunday nights, no matter what Daddy had said.

Now, though, it was time to get ready for school. Emma ran up the stairs to get her backpack and to put Marmaduke and Marshmallow back in their cage.

But when she got to her room—no ferrets.

"Where are you, you rascals?" Emma said out loud. She closed the door behind her and listened. Usually, she could find them by hearing them rustling around. But nothing. She peeked under the bed. No. She looked in the bed and under the covers. She peered inside the pillowcases.

No. She sighed. She didn't have time right now to search for them. They were always finding new, sneaky hiding places. Once Marmaduke had hidden in one of her boots. Another time, he had burrowed inside a box of dolls and had chewed up the leg of her American Girl doll. Mom had to send the doll to the doll hospital to get a whole new leg. Since then, Emma kept her dolls up high on a shelf.

She listened some more. She still didn't hear anything, no rustling, nothing. Maybe they had fallen asleep somewhere.

"It's all right," she said. "I don't know where you're hiding. But it's okay. Have fun running around all day. Just don't get into any trouble, okay?"

Emma knew they had heard her. Sometimes they played at being quiet. She'd just close her door. Mom had told her they could run free sometimes if her door were shut tight.

Emma grabbed her backpack, shut the door tight, and ran downstairs. She yelled good-bye and dashed outside to wait for the bus. Just then she remembered she hadn't returned the laptop to Daddy. Well, she figured, he'd come get it when he needed it.

On the bus, Emma kept thinking about Luisa and camping. Luisa didn't have any brothers or sisters, and she loved being with Emma's big family. Emma had missed Luisa a lot since soccer season had ended and Luisa had started to take dance lessons. Emma had just a little tiny fear inside that Luisa might have something else to do for the weekend, maybe even with Katie. She hoped not.

When Emma got into school, she found Luisa in the hallway by the cubbies. Luisa and some other kids from class were putting their stuff away. One of the kids was Jordan. Emma used to hate Jordan, but now they were kind of friends. Jordan was really, really funny. Sometimes people teased Emma that Jordan was her boyfriend. And she knew they teased Jordan, too. But neither she nor Jordan cared. They were just kind of friendly and talked on the bus once in a while.

Mrs. Adams, their teacher, was standing nearby talking to another teacher. But—hooray!—no Katie.

"Luisa!" Emma said, grabbing her hand and pulling her aside. "Wait till you hear!"

—"Wait till *you* hear!" Luisa said back. "Did you get the e-mail?"

"What e-mail?"

"Never mind," Luisa said. "Go ahead. You first."

"Okay. Guess what?" Emma said.

"What?"

"We're going camping tomorrow. And we're staying over till Saturday and maybe even Sunday."

"Oh, lucky you!"

"No, lucky *you*. Because guess what else?"

"What?" Luisa said.

"You're going with us!"

"I am?" Luisa said.

Emma nodded. "If you want. And if your mom says you can."

"Oh, cool!" Luisa said. "Oh, wow! When? Really tomorrow?"

"Yup. Because of no school."

"Oh, I hope I can go! I can't wait!" Luisa said. "I'll ask. Is everybody going? Your whole family?"

Emma nodded. "Yup. Annie, too." And that reminded Emma. "Luisa!" she said. "At the dance school where you take hip-hop, do they teach Irish dance?"

"I think so," Luisa said. "Why? I asked you to join hip-hop and you said you didn't like dance."

28

Emma shrugged. "I don't. Well, I do. A little bit. Sort of."

"Well, now, my turn," Luisa said. "Guess what about the talent show?"

Emma frowned. "What talent show?"

"You know. Didn't your parents get the e-mail from school? Mrs. Adams sent it last night."

"Oh," Emma said. "No. I guess not. I mean, I had Daddy's computer all night."

"Oh. Well, Mrs. Adams sent an e-mail about our class having a talent show. She said since she got to be Teacher of the Year, the class should have a talent show so we could show how great we are, too. But she doesn't want us to do an individual thing. It's got to be something that we do with someone else. We can do a group, or just two, like partners. You and me!"

Emma smiled. *You and me!*

"Isn't that cool?" Luisa said. "So what do we do better than anybody in the whole world?"

"Soccer?"

"No, silly. On the playground. Jump rope! We're the best Double Dutch jump ropers in the school. Remember how we jumped together for Heart Healthy Week? And the other kids couldn't even believe that we could do it at the same time? So that's what we'll do. And we need two more to turn the ropes, so we'll have lots of helpers. Maybe even some of the boys will turn. Jordan was good at it."

"Yeah!" Emma said. She smiled at Luisa. She had been silly to worry about Luisa not being her best friend anymore.

She put her lunch into her cubby, then got out her morning journal and spelling notebook. She turned around just as Katie arrived, all breathless and smiling.

Emma tried to smile back. She tried to like Katie. She really, really did. But it was hard. Katie was a big show-off. Worse, though, sometimes she was nice, and other times, super mean. And you could never tell which Katie would turn up.

"Oh, Luisa, Emma!" Katie cried out. "Isn't it great about the talent show? I have so much to tell you!" She waved at Mrs. Adams. "Mrs. Adams!" she said. "This is the best idea!"

Mrs. Adams smiled at Katie before turning and going into the classroom.

"So listen!" Katie said. "Wait till you hear! Mrs. Thomas, my dance teacher—I mean, *our* dance teacher, right, Luisa?—anyway, she called last night. She said I'm going to have a starring role in the dance concert. In *five* dances! Isn't that cool?"

"Oh," Luisa said. "Wow. It is. It's . . . cool."

But Emma thought that Luisa looked a little mad. Or maybe sad. Emma didn't blame her. If she were Luisa, she wouldn't think it was so cool. How could she? Katie and Luisa were both in the same dance class.

As usual, Katie didn't seem to have a clue about what Luisa might be feeling. She took Luisa's arm. "And that's not all," she went on. "You know that dance we do together, how we kick out toward each other with that high kick? I asked if we could do that, and she said maybe. She said maybe it could even be the opening number if we practice enough!"

"Really?" Luisa said. Her eyes got wide. "Did she really say that? Honest? You're not making it up?"

"Honest!" Katie said. "And it's going to be perfect for the school talent show, too, because . . ." She stopped. She looked at Emma. She turned back to Luisa. "Later," she said softly.

Emma could feel her face get hot. "Well, that's rude!" she said.

"Oh, I'm sorry," Katie said sweetly—fake sweetly, Emma thought. "I just didn't want you to feel left out." She turned to Luisa again. "That dance is perfect for the talent show because it takes two of us. We'll do it together."

31

"Oh," Luisa said.

"Okay?" Katie said.

Luisa didn't answer. She stared down at her feet. She shrugged. "Uh. I don't know," she said. "I mean . . ."

She looked at Emma.

Emma's heart was thumping hard. Would Luisa back out of her promise? Would she rather dance with Katie?

Maybe she was thinking what Emma herself was thinking—that hip-hop dance would be a whole lot more fun, and a whole lot cooler, than jumping rope.

Chapter Five
Emma Breaks a Big, Big Rule

The bell rang and everyone hurried into the classroom. Luisa scooted away without another word or another look at Emma. They all sat down in their seats. Luisa's desk was right next to Emma's, and Katie's was behind Luisa's. Emma saw Katie lean forward and whisper something to Luisa. Luisa didn't answer, but she shook her head.

What had Katie whispered? *Will you do hip-hop with me?* Had Luisa said *No, I won't?* Or what?

It took Mrs. Adams a long time to get the class calmed down, since everybody was buzzing about the talent show. It wasn't until Mrs. Adams said it was time to write in their personal journals that people got quiet. During personal journal time, you weren't allowed to ask questions or talk or anything. You couldn't even get up to sharpen your pencil. Mrs. Adams made everybody do that before they started writing. And then they had to write for fifteen whole minutes. Even Mrs. Adams wrote during that time.

The class was supposed to write about feelings and thoughts and important things. Mrs. Adams promised that she would never read their journals, so they could write whatever they wanted. Emma knew that teachers were mostly honest, Mrs. Adams, especially. Still, just in case, Emma never wrote about school or anything important at all. Instead, she made things up. Like she wrote about how she was allowed to pilot planes with Daddy. And she wrote about how Marmaduke won a contest for best-looking ferret and was going to be in an ad for pet food. Sometimes she just doodled around on the pages, drawing pictures of dogs and stuff, or just wrote her name with special kinds of lettering. Today, there was plenty to write about if she wanted to—her worries about Luisa and the talent show and stupid show-off Katie. And her really big worry—Annie and Bo.

She sighed and stared at her journal.

She glanced over at Luisa. Luisa's head was bent over her journal, and she was frowning as she wrote. What was she writing? Was she sorry she had said she'd do jump rope with Emma? Had she changed her mind?

Emma peeked at Katie. Katie was writing furiously. What was *she* writing? Was she plotting how she could get Luisa to dance with her?

Emma sighed and picked up her pencil. It was hard to write because she had to rest her scraped-up right arm on the desk and she was right handed. She tried using her left hand.

Wow. That was creepy. She could hardly even make any letters. It was fun to try, though, even though it took like five whole minutes just to write her name.

And then the intercom buzzed with a message about Luisa and a dentist appointment or something. Mrs. Adams called Luisa up to her desk. And just like that, a little thought crept into Emma's head. She took a quick look around the room. She knew how to find out what Luisa was thinking . . . was writing. About dance. And jump rope. And best friends.

But no. She couldn't do that. It wouldn't be nice. Or fair. Luisa was her best friend.

But Luisa would never know. Nobody would know. Everyone was writing, heads bent over their journals. All Emma could hear was the scratching of pens and pencils on paper.

She swallowed hard. She couldn't help herself. She leaned out to the left of her desk. And peeked at Luisa's journal.

She saw writing, super neat writing, slanting back, as if it were about to fall backward off the page. But it was so slanted that Emma had trouble reading it. She tilted her head to see better. She could read a line—half a line. *I wish Mom let me . . .*

Emma squinted. Let her, what? *Go camping?* Oh, yea, Luisa wanted to go camping with her!

She leaned her head farther out. There, she could see more now.

. . . let me have sparkly nail polish, but she says not till I'm twelve. . . .

Bam! Emma jumped.

Katie had leaped to her feet and had come up next to her. She slammed her hand down hard, shutting Luisa's journal.

"Mrs. Adams!" Katie yelled. "Mrs. Adams! Emma was reading Luisa's journal!"

Emma straightened up in her seat. She made herself look innocent. "That's a lie!" she said.

"Is not!" Katie cried.

Emma looked at Luisa standing at Mrs. Adams's desk. Luisa blinked at her. She looked as though her dog had just been run over by a truck.

"Emma?" Mrs. Adams said quietly. "Were you?"

Emma swallowed hard. She could feel her face get hot. Not innocent looking.

"She was, Mrs. Adams!" Katie said. "I saw her. I

saw her. She was leaning over so she could read—"

"Okay, Katie," Mrs. Adams interrupted. "Calm down. Luisa, go sit. Your mom's coming to get you at lunchtime for the dentist, so copy the homework assignment off the board. And, Emma, you come with me." She pointed to the door. "The rest of you," she said, "go on with your journals. And keep your eyes to yourselves."

Emma pushed her desk chair back, tears crowding into her eyes. Now Luisa would be mad at her. And she'd dance in the talent show with Katie. And it was all Katie's fault.

Except it wasn't. Emma knew that. It was *her* fault. She shouldn't have been reading Luisa's journal. Still, she hadn't done it to be mean. It was just that she had been so worried.

Emma got to her feet. She hated having to go out into the hall. It meant you were in trouble. It meant you'd get a big fat lecture. Maybe even a note home—or an e-mail sent to your parents. As if she didn't have enough trouble. Mostly, it was bad kids who got called out into the hall. Like Jordan. Jordan wasn't really bad, though. Not like Katie. Jordan would never tell on her.

Now, Emma glanced at him. He gave her an "I'm sorry" look.

She turned to Luisa. Luisa seemed mad, super

mad. Katie was smirking. Emma looked away.

Out in the hall, Mrs. Adams put her hand on Emma's shoulder. She did it gently, but she bent close to Emma's face, very serious seeming.

"Emma," she said, "tell me the truth. Were you reading Luisa's journal?"

Emma stared down at her feet. What could she say? She could tell the truth. And get in trouble. Or she could lie. And not get in trouble.

Or . . . she could tell pretty much the truth. She took a deep breath.

"See," she said, "I hurt my arm, my right arm. And I was having trouble writing. So I was trying to use my left hand to write, so I was leaning over to that side. I was. So I was *kind* of reading it. But I didn't mean to. It's just that I looked over, and it was right there and—"

Mrs. Adams held up her hand. "But you know the rules of privacy. Even if it were open and right by your desk, you shouldn't have read it. I'm surprised at you. How would you feel if someone read *your* personal journal?"

Emma shrugged.

"I want you to think about it," Mrs. Adams said. "Think how you'd feel if someone read your personal thoughts. You know we teach respect for one another in this class. I hope you'll see fit to apologize to Luisa later. And apologize to Katie, too, for saying she was lying."

Apologize to Katie? Fat chance. But to Luisa— yes. Emma knew she should. She nodded.

"And I want you to stay in at recess to think about the importance of respecting another person's privacy," Mrs. Adams said.

"No!" Emma said. She *needed* to be out on the playground. She *needed* to say I'm sorry to Luisa. Right away. Before Katie could steal Luisa away! "No!" Emma said again. "I have to say I'm sorry to Luisa! At recess. This morning! I have to say it right away."

"Well," Mrs. Adams said. "I'm glad you want to apologize. But you think for a while first. You can apologize later. Now let's go back to class."

Back in the classroom, Mrs. Adams wrote Emma's name in the "restricted privileges" place on the board. Everyone knew what that meant— no recess. Emma slid into her seat, her head bent, feeling all hot and embarrassed. It was so not fair!

For the rest of the morning, Emma kept glancing over toward Luisa. She so much wanted to at least give Luisa an "I'm sorry" look. But Luisa kept her head buried in a book and wouldn't even raise her eyes to Emma.

Later that morning, after silent reading, there

was horrible spelling. Emma couldn't spell for anything and she got six out of ten wrong on the spelling test. And she *had* studied! And then it was time for recess—the best time of the day.

The worst time of the day.

People got coats and sweaters and stuff from their cubbies in the hall, then came back in the room and lined up.

Emma stayed in her seat, staring down at her desk, fighting tears that kept creeping into her eyes. The one time she raised her head, she saw that Luisa and Katie were lined up side by side. Katie whispered something to Luisa, and this time, Luisa nodded back.

Emma wondered if Luisa had chosen dance. And Katie.

Emma slumped down in her seat.

After a minute or so, everybody began filing out of the classroom, heading for the playground. As Jordan went by, he dropped something on Emma's desk, a tiny square of folded-up paper.

Emma unfolded it. It was a note. It said, "Katie stinks."

Emma looked up at him. He grinned.

Nobody else looked at her.

Not even Luisa.

Chapter Six
Annie to the Rescue

There wasn't even Tim to talk to on the bus going home, and Emma needed him. Big time. He was the only person she could tell about the rotten things that had happened. But it was his music lesson day, and on music lesson days, he rode the activity bus home. Emma decided to take a seat right behind the bus driver so nobody would bother her. Most people stayed as far away from the driver as possible, so they could fool around. But just as Emma was about to sit down, she tripped over her backpack. Her books spilled everywhere. Jordan helped her pick them up, but some of the other boys laughed. Not only that, but when she scrambled after her books, she bumped her scraped-up arm.

Finally, after she got her backpack together again, she sat and stared out the window, thinking.

Annie knew how to help with friends. Mom was good with friends, too, but Annie was better. Annie had helped Emma once before when Katie was being a pain on the soccer field. And once, Annie had a great idea about fixing things with Jordan when Emma had accidentally gotten Jordan into trouble.

And now Emma really needed help! Luisa had left for the dentist right after morning recess and before lunch, so Emma hadn't had a chance to try to explain. She also hadn't had a chance to talk to Luisa more about camping—if Luisa still wanted to go, that is. And camping was tomorrow!

When Emma got off the bus, she walked slowly up the sidewalk. It was late fall, but a warm, sunny day, and she kicked leaves as she went. She looked at the driveway that curved around in front of her house. There were no cars. Mom and Daddy were gone. Bo's car wasn't there either, his little rusted-out car that sounded like a lawn mower—a very loud lawn mower. Emma could always hear it coming from blocks away. She was very glad he wasn't around.

Now, as Emma turned up the walk, she saw Annie—Annie sitting on the steps waiting for her. Like she had known that Emma needed to talk to her right this very minute.

Annie held out her arms. "Hey, sweetie!" she called. "Come give me a hug. It's just you and me today."

"Where's everybody?" Emma asked. She dumped her backpack, jumped up the steps, and plopped down beside Annie. She leaned into Annie's side, feeling how good it was to be alone with her—just the two of them together.

"Your mom's at a meeting in the city," Annie said. "Your daddy took the little ones off for a while. Woof, too." Annie laughed. "They were begging for 'Daddy time.' I think they really wanted ice cream. You know how your daddy is."

Emma nodded. She did know. Daddy loved ice cream and he also loved spoiling the kids. Emma knew he missed them a lot when he was on one of his piloting trips. She also knew how much Woof loved ice cream. He always got his own dish of vanilla when they went to Mr. Mike's.

"So it's just us!" Annie said. "You and me. What would you like to do on this beautiful afternoon?"

"Talk!" Emma said, straightening up and looking at Annie.

Annie laughed. "That's all?"

"No, it's not all. But let's do that first. I have to talk to you about Luisa. And this."

She pushed up her sleeve and showed Annie her

43

arm. The scrape had been healing as the day went on, until she'd bumped it in the bus.

"Ouch!" Annie said. "That must hurt. How'd you do that?"

"I fell."

"Well, we'll clean it up and put some Band-Aids on it. How did you fall?"

Emma looked away. "On the bus," she said. That was true. Sort of true. Even if it wasn't the whole truth. Which she could not tell. About spying on Annie.

But then she did tell the truth—the true story of the day—no lies, just the truth about the whole rotten day. She told about how she never saw Luisa anymore and how Katie and Luisa were in hip-hop dance together and were like best friends now. She told how Katie was being such a jerk and how Emma had gotten in trouble because Katie told on her. And Emma told the truth about reading Luisa's journal. She told, too, why she had read it and what she wanted to find out.

Annie put her arm around Emma and nodded every once in a while. When Emma was all finished, Annie hugged her close. "Oh, me dear," she said softly. "It's so hard to be a kid, isn't it?"

"It is!" Emma said, pulling away and looking up at Annie. "Annie, what should I do?"

"Well," Annie said slowly, "I can think of a few things. But let's start with the easy one."

"There isn't an easy one," Emma said.

"Oh, but there is. You have to take dance lessons, too."

"I do?" Emma said. And then she added, "Exactly! That's exactly what I've been thinking." Of course, she had been—but not for the reason Annie thought. "I want to learn Irish dance," she said. "I love dance contests. Like the one you're going to be in next week."

"*Irish dance?*" Annie said. "You said your friends were in hip-hop."

"Yeah. But I think Irish dance would be better."

"And how would that help with friends?"

Emma leaned against Annie again. She sighed. It wouldn't. But if she learned Irish dance, she could go with Annie on dance nights. Bo would hate having her around, she was sure. She looked at Annie's wrist. Annie was wearing the stupid Bo bracelet. It wasn't even that pretty, just a bunch of pink and green beads, but Annie never took it off.

"Anyway," Emma said, "only *one* of them is my friend. And she's been taking lessons for weeks and weeks."

"So?" Annie said. "You can learn hip-hop in a hurry. Anyone who can run around a soccer field

45

the way you do can tear up a dance floor. So let's forget Irish dance, shall we? And we'll see if your mum and dad will let you take hip-hop."

Emma stared down at her feet. Weird. She knew joining Irish dance wasn't going to help with Luisa. And hip-hop could. Or might. But then, what about Annie? And Bo? A real dilemma.

"Daddy already said no to dance," Emma said.

"I know," Annie said. "But sometimes your mum and dad change their minds. If there's a good enough reason." She smiled at Emma. "Dance is really wonderful exercise. It's not like sitting in front of a computer all day."

Emma giggled. Like she *ever* did that! But she knew what Annie was trying to say.

"Come, now!" Annie said, standing up and pulling Emma to her feet. "Here's my idea—first we get your arm cleaned up. Then, since the wee ones are getting ice cream, surely you'll need some, too."

"Okay," Emma said. And then she remembered something. "But wait, I have to take care of Marmaduke and Marshmallow. I left them loose in my room today."

"You do that," Annie said, "while I go get the Band-Aids."

As they went into the house together, Emma felt

a little happier, and not just because of what Annie said. It was because she'd had a thought—maybe she could take two kinds of dance, Irish and hip-hop both! That could be cool, couldn't it? But would Mom and Daddy let her? Maybe. Like Annie said, sometimes they changed their minds if there was a good reason.

Emma ran upstairs. But at the door to her room, she stopped short. Her bedroom door was open. Open! Emma knew she had closed it that morning. Then what . . . ?

She hurried into her room. She looked around. "Marmaduke! Marshmallow!" she called softly. She listened.

Nothing. No rustling around. No sound at all.

Where were they? How did the door get open? And then she remembered—Daddy! The laptop. She looked at the window seat. The laptop was gone. Had Daddy maybe put Marmaduke and Marshmallow back in their cage? She looked. No. The cage was empty.

But Daddy wouldn't leave the door open! He knew better. Then it had to be one of the little kids. They were always sneaking into her room without permission!

Emma peeked under the bed. She looked in her closet. She looked in all the ferrets' favorite hiding

47

places—her doll clothes box, her boots, inside the pillowcases. They were nowhere.

Emma sucked in a big breath. Well, she wasn't going to get too crazy. They'd disappeared lots of times before, and always they got found. Maybe she'd just wait till Woof came home. He was great at sniffing them out and then chasing after them all around the house, making a big game of it.

Emma ran down the stairs to the kitchen. "Annie!" she said. "Guess what? Marmaduke and Marshmallow are gone."

Annie was at the table with some Band-Aids and lotion for cleaning cuts. "Gone?" she said. "Oh, dear!"

She signaled for Emma to come to her. Emma held out her arm, and Annie began cleaning it up.

"How did they get out, I wonder," Annie said.

"I let them out of their cage this morning, and I know I closed the door tight," Emma said. "But Daddy came and got his laptop, and maybe he left the door open. Or else one of the little kids did. Were they in my room today?"

"I don't think so," Annie said.

"Annie?" Emma said. "I really want to go get ice cream."

"We're going," Annie said. "Just as soon as I put this next Band-Aid on."

"I know," Emma said. "But I mean, do you think I should look for Marmaduke and Marshmallow first?"

"We could," Annie said. "If you're worried. But I'm not worried. You know they always turn up. They're in this house somewhere. Why don't we just get ice cream, and we'll round them up when we get back?"

Emma nodded. "Okay," she said. "Maybe I'll make Daddy find them." She giggled, remembering. "Once Marmaduke was even inside Mom and Daddy's mattress. That really scared Daddy. Mom, too."

Annie laughed. "We'll pray to the good saints that those rascals aren't in anybody's mattress now. Like mine!" She finished patting the last Band-Aid into place. "Okay, me dear," she said. "You're all fixed up. Shall we go?"

"Okay," Emma said. "Thanks. My arm feels better."

Emma started toward the back door. As she opened it, a gray streak whizzed past her, almost tripping her.

Marmaduke! Marshmallow! One of them, flying between her feet. Out the door. Down the steps. Across the back lawn.

Gone.

49

Chapter Seven

Marmaduke Is Gone!

It was late day, almost nighttime, and practically completely dark. A few stars were just peeking out of the navy blue sky.

And Marmaduke was still missing. Missing in the out of doors.

Marshmallow had been found. When Daddy got home with Woof, Woof had sniffed Marshmallow out from her hiding place—inside the piano! Now she was safely back in her cage with water and food.

But Marmaduke was nowhere to be found.

Everybody in the house had been searching since they got home—Emma and Annie and Mom and Daddy and Tim and even the little kids. Daddy kept saying how sorry he was, that he was sure he had closed Emma's door tightly after getting the computer. Emma felt bad for him. But she couldn't say that it was all right. It wasn't all right! *Somebody* had left her door open. Emma wanted to be mad at the little kids, because she thought it was probably one of them. But McClain and the twins were all working so hard, looking everywhere, that she couldn't really feel mad at them. Mom kept telling Emma that Marmaduke was smart, that he was sure to find his way back and not to worry so much. But Emma could tell from the way Mom was frowning and biting her lip that she was pretty worried, too.

They searched and searched. Ira and Lizzie got down on their hands and knees and crawled under bushes and peeked around rocks. McClain and Tim got very brave and together went down to the creek behind the house. Annie went with them. Nobody ever went there because once Tim said he saw snakes there. Today, they didn't see any snakes. But they didn't see Marmaduke either.

Emma searched the front yard, the backyard, and all around each side of the house. Alongside the garage, too. Everywhere. Daddy put Woof on a leash, and Woof led Daddy all over the yard. But the only things Woof sniffed out were one rabbit, a fat squirrel, and two squeaky chipmunks.

Emma was half crazy with worry. Marmaduke had never been missing this long and never in the dark. And only once had he gotten outside, but that was just for a second or two.

At dinnertime, Mom insisted that they all come in and sit down to eat together. But how could Emma eat? How could anybody eat? Even the little kids were worried and sad and just picked at their food. And it was spaghetti, too!

Annie sat down with them, though usually she went to her own apartment at dinnertime. Lately, Emma had noticed that Bo came and picked her up, and they went out to dinner together. Annie wasn't eating either, though, just sitting and twirling her bead bracelet 'round and 'round, her face worried and upset looking.

All through dinner, nobody spoke. People just picked up forks, then put them down. Somebody asked for the bread. Somebody else asked for the grated cheese. But then nobody ate anything. Lizzie knocked over a glass of milk and started to cry. That made Ira cry, too. Annie jumped to her feet and got a bunch of paper towels and mopped things up.

"Thanks, Annie," Mom said.

Then everyone got quiet again.

Emma thought about her day. Her rotten, awful, terrible day. At school, she had thought things couldn't get worse. Only now, they had. A whole lot worse.

Emma was just about to ask if she could go out looking again, when McClain spoke up.

"Know what?" McClain said, sounding all bright and happy. "I know something to make you feel happy, Emma."

Emma just shrugged. As if anything could!

"What's that, McClain?" Daddy said.

"It's all right," McClain said. "It's not so bad. Because Emma still has Marshmallow!"

"That's stupid, McClain!" Emma said, glaring at her.

"Emma!" Mom said, a warning sound in her voice. But she didn't sound too mad.

"But it was! It was stupid to say that," Emma cried. "She thinks that Marshmallow can take Marmaduke's place! It's like he's . . . he's . . . like he's—"

"Not important!" Tim said. "Replaceable."

"Right!" Emma said. "You don't just throw him away and get another one. How would you like it if we threw you away?"

She glared across the table at McClain. And she felt tears well up.

McClain looked down at her plate. "I just meant . . . I didn't mean . . ." And then she looked as if she were going to cry, too.

Mom reached over and ruffled McClain's curls.

53

"It's all right, sweetie," she said. "We know what you meant."

"Emma doesn't," McClain said.

"Emma's just sad," Mom said.

"Me, too," Ira said. "I like Marmaduke."

"Me, too," Lizzie said. "Even though he bited me once."

"Bit you once," McClain said.

"That's what I said," Lizzie said. She looked at Ira. "Didn't he, Ira?"

Ira nodded.

Again, everybody got quiet. And then in the silence, Emma heard something. Something loud. Something rattling and roaring. Something stupid. Bo's stupid car.

Emma looked at Annie.

Annie pushed her chair back and stood up. "Excuse me, please," she said. She went into the hall, opened the front door, and disappeared into the dark.

Emma couldn't sit there one more minute. "I'm going outside to look some more, okay?" she said.

"You've hardly eaten anything," Mom said.

Emma shrugged.

Mom looked at Daddy.

Daddy nodded.

"I'll come out with you in a minute, Emma," Daddy said.

"All right," Mom said. "I'll come, too. But we can't look for long. It's already pitch dark. And before you go out, I want you to go upstairs and get your warm jacket."

"Okay," Emma said.

She went into the hall and started up the stairs. It was dark in the hall, but she didn't even bother to turn on the light. She was halfway up the stairs, when behind her, the front door burst open.

"Emma!" Annie called. "Emma, look who's here!"

Emma turned and looked down.

Bo. Big deal. Bo was there, tall, skinny Bo, standing alongside Annie. He was wearing a bulgy denim jacket, and his wild yellow hair was sprouting all over the place. He looked like the Scarecrow from *The Wizard of Oz*. Even though the hall was dark, Emma could see that he was smiling up at her.

"And will you look who I found!" Bo said, smiling even wider. "Just ambling along the driveway! Waiting for someone to scoop him up!"

He opened his bulgy jacket. And there, snuggled up against his chest, was a very dirty, very wet, very ratty-looking ferret.

Marmaduke!

Emma flew down the stairs, jumping the last three steps completely. She ran across the hall and snatched Marmaduke out of Bo's arms. "Oh, you're home. You came home!" she cried, and she kissed the top of his head. "Oh, I'm so happy. You're home."

She hugged Marmaduke to her. He was all wet and slimy feeling, and his little heart was going *thump, thump, thump*, hard and fast, as though he'd been so scared.

She looked at Bo. "You found him!" she whispered. "Oh, thank you. Thank you so, so much. You found him!"

Bo ducked his head, seeming kind of shy and embarrassed. "It was my pleasure," he said softly. "He's very sweet, isn't he?"

"He is!" Emma said. And suddenly, she was so very happy and so grateful, that she had the strangest feeling—she felt like hugging Bo! She really, really did. Only thing was, her arms were full of Marmaduke.

Besides, Bo was hugging Annie.

Chapter Eight
Going Camping

It was the next morning. Marmaduke was home and safe and cozy in his cage. The family was scurrying around, getting ready to go camping. The little kids had lugged their pillows and blankets downstairs so the bedding could be loaded into the van. McClain had her blanket wrapped around her head, pretending to be a princess. Ira and Lizzie had theirs flung around their shoulders like capes. They said they were superheroes. Tim was outside helping Daddy load the tent and tent poles and camping stove into the van. In the kitchen, Mom was getting ice and hot dogs and juices to put in the ice chest.

And Emma was standing at the door to the kitchen, fuming mad. Mad, mad, mad. Everything was wrong. Absolutely everything. Last night, she had called Luisa to tell her she was sorry for reading her journal. Luisa's mother said Luisa was sleeping. Luisa had had a tooth that was coming in on top of another tooth, and the dentist had to pull the old tooth. Her jaw was all swollen, and she was taking medicine and it made her sleepy. And so she couldn't come to the phone—and she couldn't go camping either!

Of course, Emma felt sad for Luisa. But she was worried, too. Was Luisa really that sick? Or was she just a little bit sick but didn't want to go camping because she was still mad?

And then, a much worse thing happened. Mom announced at breakfast that *Bo was coming on the camping trip, too!*

"Why does he have to come with us?" Emma asked now, for about the hundredth time.

Mom looked up from the ice chest and sighed. "Why not?" she asked. For about the hundredth time.

"Because!" Emma said.

Mom wiped her hands on a towel, then came and put an arm around Emma's shoulders. "Emma, dear," she said. "What is it? Do you really dislike Bo so much?"

"Yes. I do. I can't stand him."

"But why? Daddy and I think he's a very appealing

young man. What don't you like about him?"

"Everything."

"He found Marmaduke for you," Mom said, hugging Emma closer.

"I'd have found Marmaduke myself!" Emma said, ducking away from Mom's arm and glaring at her. "If Marmaduke was just plain walking up the driveway like Bo said, then I'd have found him as soon as I got my jacket."

"Emma, you're being silly," Mom said. "Bo is coming with us, and I expect that you'll be perfectly gracious to him. Now go upstairs and get your things together. And don't forget a warm sweatshirt. No, better bring two. It's going to be cold, I think."

Emma started out of the room, but at the door, she stopped and turned back. She was so mad she could spit. "Mom!" she said.

"Enough!" Mom said.

"No! Listen," Emma said. "There's no *room* in the tent for Bo. Our tent is crowded. And it will be even more crowded because of Annie. So where's Bo going to sleep?"

"Not to worry," Mom said, smiling. "Bo is an experienced backpacker. He told us that last night. He's hiked all over the Appalachian Trail. He has his own one-person pup tent, and he'll set it up right next to ours. So there will be plenty of room in our tent for our whole family, and for Annie, too. I think it will be great fun."

"Well, *I* think it will be stupid. That's what I think!" Emma said.

And she stomped her way up to her room. As if anyone cared what she thought!

Emma got her backpack and began throwing things in—two books, her favorite sweatshirts, some candy that she had left over from Halloween. Why did Bo have to come along? Why couldn't Mom and Daddy see how much he was taking over Annie's life? And time?

There was only one thing to do—follow through with her plan. Be a big pest and don't let Annie and Bo have a minute alone together, and do it constantly for two whole days. By the end of the camping trip, they would be sick of her. Bo would probably be mad at Annie, too, because of Emma hanging around all the time. Because Emma knew that Annie wouldn't ever tell her to go away.

After a while, everything was packed and the whole family climbed into the van, Annie and Bo, too. The van was big and nine people fit in easily. The twins sat in their car seats in their usual second row, just behind Mom and Daddy. There was a little TV there, and on long rides it kept all the kids happy—except for the times that they fought over what to watch. Tim and McClain got in the next row of seats, Tim with his ear buds stuck in his ears so he could listen to his iPod. And Emma took a seat in the way back row. She scrambled in fast, taking the middle spot, so that she'd be between Annie and Bo. That way, they couldn't hold hands or anything with her mashed there between them.

When they were all buckled in, they set off for the state park. It was only about an hour away, but it always seemed to Emma as if it were a deep, deep forest hundreds of miles away. There were trees and streams and cliffs and chipmunks and rabbits and raccoons and deer. Once, they had seen a mother fox with a baby kit. McClain, of course, wanted to keep the baby fox and the mother fox, too. There was even a sign at the entrance to the park that warned campers to be on the lookout for bears. But nobody had ever seen a bear, and Daddy said he thought the sign was a big exaggeration. And besides, Daddy said, there was nothing to worry about because bears were more scared of people than people were scared of bears.

"So, Emma," Bo said, once they had started out, "what do you like best about camping?"

Emma shrugged. "Lots of stuff."

"Like what, for instance?" Bo asked.

"Just . . . stuff," Emma answered.

She didn't want to be rude, but she didn't want to be friendly, either. And she was so far in the back, and with the TV on, Mom and Daddy probably couldn't hear if she were being rude.

"Want me to tell you what I like best?" Bo asked.

"If you have to," Emma said.

"Okay," Bo said. "My favorite part is the wildlife. When I was a kid growing up in Montana, my friends and I would go camping. We'd sit quietly around the campfire at night, and some nights, if we were quiet enough, foxes and coyotes and other wildlife came right up close."

"Foxes don't scare me," Emma said. "I've seen them before."

"They didn't scare us, either," Bo said. "They stayed just far enough away that we could see their eyes lit up by the campfire. They watched us, and we watched them, all of us quiet and still. It was just amazing."

"Emma?" Annie said. "Know what? Bo loves animals, just the way you do. Did you know that he's studying to be a vet?"

"It's probably not that hard to do," Emma said.

"It takes a long while, though," Bo said. "I still have three more years of study."

"You'll be old by then," Emma said.

Bo laughed. "Not that old."

"I'm going to be a vet, too," McClain said, turning around in her seat.

"Really?" Bo said.

"I'm going to work with Dr. Pete," McClain said. "And I'm going to take care of just kitties. Maybe puppies, too. I'm not sure."

"I'm going to work with big animals," Bo said.

"Like Woof?" McClain asked.

"Even bigger," Bo said. "Horses and cows, actually."

"Cows!" Emma said. "Gross." She knew she was being horrible. But she couldn't help herself.

"What about bears?" McClain asked. "Will you take care of them? Did they come to your campfire?"

Bo shook his head. "No. But I met up with a bear once on the Appalachian Trail. It was very scary. Believe me, I don't mess with bears."

"There're bears where we're going," Emma said. "The sign says so."

"I hope not," Bo said.

"Are you scared of them?" Emma asked.

Bo nodded. "I am."

"What would you do if you saw one?" McClain asked. "At the campground?"

"Run screaming!" Bo said. "Or climb a tree."

"But you'd rescue me first," Annie said.

"Nope!" Bo said, laughing.

Annie frowned. "And I thought you were my hero," she said. "Not afraid of anything."

Emma knew that Annie and Bo were both teasing. Still, she had a feeling that Annie was at least a little bit serious.

Bo reached across the seat behind Emma and laid a hand on Annie's shoulder. "Actually," he said, "there's only one thing that I'm really afraid of."

"What?" Emma asked.

Bo didn't answer. And when Emma looked from Bo to Annie, she saw that they were smiling at one another, one of those secret kinds of smiles.

"What?" Emma asked again. "Bears?"

"No," Bo said softly, but he was speaking to Annie. "Losing you. Having something—or someone—come between us."

They kept on looking at one another, Annie's eyes all dreamy like.

"That won't happen," Annie said.

Yuck.

It took a few more seconds, but finally the two of them stopped with the yucky looks. Bo laughed, and Annie took Emma's hand.

"Emma, sweetie," she said. "Bo and I were just

teasing. There are no bears. Don't be scared."

I'm not. But Bo is, Emma thought.

"I'm not scared," McClain said.

"Good girl!" Bo said. "Me, neither. Because if there were really bears in this park, someone would have seen them. And nobody has. Right?"

"Right," McClain said.

Right, Emma thought. And she smiled to herself.

But there's always a first time.

Chapter Nine
McClain Tags Along

Once they got to the campsite and unloaded the van, Daddy handed out jobs—big jobs for the big kids and little jobs for the little ones to keep them at the campsite so they wouldn't wander away and get lost.

At first, Daddy assigned Annie and Bo the job of going farther into the woods to find dry firewood and kindling for the campfire. But Bo suggested he stay and help Daddy and Tim set up the tent since the tent was really heavy.

"I'll go with Annie!" Emma said. "I'll go!"

"Okay," Daddy said. "You two can go. Remember to get dry twigs and sticks, though. Really dry."

"We will!" Emma said. "Won't we, Annie?"

"Count on us!" Annie said.

Emma grabbed a couple of canvas bags for the firewood, and she and Annie started down the path into the woods. Annie carried a huge flashlight since it would be dark soon. They hadn't gone more than a few steps, when McClain came barreling up behind. "Wait up!" she cried. "Wait up!"

Emma whirled around. "No, McClain!" she said. "Daddy gave you another job."

"He said I should unroll the sleeping bags," McClain said. "I already did."

"How could you?" Emma said. "He hasn't even set up the tent yet!"

"I put them under the trees," McClain said. "I'm finished."

"Then go help the twins!" Emma said.

"Oh, me dear!" Annie said, reaching for Emma's hand and squeezing it. "We don't mind sharing, do we?"

"Yes! We do! I mean, I do."

And she did. She wanted to be with Annie alone, to talk about important stuff, like dance. But if she even mentioned dance, McClain would be sure to pipe up and say that Daddy had already said no. McClain never forgot anything. And she had a big mouth, too.

"Mom says you should share," McClain said. "I share with you."

"You do not!"

"Do, too. I share Kelley. I let you pet her."

"Well, I don't want to share Annie," Emma said. And then she felt really bad for saying that, even though it was true. At least, she felt bad about saying it out loud.

"That's mean," McClain said. She ducked her chin into her neck. "I wanted to see a rabbit," she said quietly. "Or a baby fox." And then, much to Emma's surprise, McClain said, "Okay," and turned away, heading back toward the campsite.

"I'll go with her and see that she gets back," Annie said.

"Never mind, I'll do it," Emma said.

She took a few steps after McClain, who was walking up the path, kicking pebbles in front of her. She looked awfully little.

"McClain!" Emma called. "All right, okay! Come on back. But you'd better not tell. . . . Oh, never mind. You can come."

"I can? Yippee!" McClain said. She turned and ran back down the path. She plopped a kiss on the sleeve of Emma's coat, then scooted ahead and scrambled up on top of some rocks. She moved so fast, she looked like a rabbit herself.

"That was sweet of you," Annie said, smiling at Emma. "You're a good big sister. Now, we need to go tell your mom and dad that she's with us."

"Maybe she told already," Emma said. She called out, "McClain? Did you tell Mom or Daddy you were coming with us?"

McClain didn't answer. Emma knew what that meant. She hadn't. "Then come with me so we can go back and tell them," Emma yelled.

"I told," McClain answered in a small voice. But from the way she said it, Emma knew very well she hadn't.

Annie laughed. "I'll go back and tell them. You two wait here. I'll be back in two seconds."

And she went running away up the path.

"Look!" McClain said when Annie was gone. "Look, Emma, look at me. I'm the Lion King!" She had climbed even higher on the boulder by the path and was crouched over on all fours, her shoulders hunched like a lion ready to pounce.

"Yeah," Emma said. "But you're too little to be the Lion King. You look more like Kelley."

"Kelley?" McClain said. "No way. I'm the Lion King. See?" She crept along the rock, her face scrunched up in a mean look, her fingers curled into claws.

"Silly you," Emma said, but she said it kindly.

Just then Annie reappeared, slightly out of breath from running. "I told them. It's all right," she said. And then she looked up at McClain. "You be careful up there, missy." She stepped closer to the rock. "Now why don't you come down?"

"Can't!" McClain said. "I'm the Lion King! You want to climb up, too, Emma? I'll let you be the Lion King if you want and I'll be—"

"No!" Emma said. "Now stop it. I don't want to be Lion King! I want to stay down here and talk to Annie."

"Okay," McClain said. "Okay, okay!"

"*Okay!*" Emma said back. Why had she ever said yes to McClain coming along?

"Annie," Emma said, trying to speak softly so that McClain wouldn't hear. "Annie, you know that Irish dance? Could I . . ."

But McClain did hear. "I can do Irish dance. Want to see? Watch!" She scrambled to her feet and started bopping up and down on top of the boulder and spinning around.

"Oh, McClain!" Annie said. She stepped over the little muddy stream that ran alongside the path. "Come down here, little one." She held up her arms. "If you fall from there, you'll break your arm, you will."

McClain threw herself into Annie's arms, so hard that Annie had to take a step backward to keep her balance. Annie swung her to the ground.

"Daddy always says I'll break my neck," McClain

said. She freed herself from Annie's arms and ran away down the path, splashing mud as she went. But she had hardly gone a few steps before she was yelling again. "Emma! Come on! I found a great hiding spot."

"Then go hide in it!" Emma yelled back.

Annie laughed. "Aren't sisters a wonder now?" she said. "When I visited me sisters a few weeks ago, we did some Irish step dancing, just like we used to when we were wee ones."

"Is that what it's called?" Emma asked. "Step dancing?"

Annie smiled. "Yes, step dancing and ceili. When we were little, we'd perform for our mum and dad in the kitchen. We pretended they were the audience. Dad said, since he was the audience, he should pay us. And he did. He always had coins and chocolates in his pockets for us." She sighed. "Dad was my hero. He was a big, strong man, not afraid of anything. And yet he was so gentle. You should have seen him with the little lambs that me sisters and I raised. And he could dance, too. He was so graceful for a big man. I miss him. Miss them all."

They were both quiet for a while as they walked on, bending occasionally to pick up dry twigs and sticks. Emma stared at the ground, worried feeling.

Annie sounded sad. Emma knew Annie missed her family a lot, even though she had just come back from visiting her sisters in Ireland. So if Annie were lonely for her family, maybe she needed a friend, a special friend. Like Bo. So maybe Emma shouldn't try and get in the way. On Sunday nights, at least.

But no, Annie had family here—their family, the whole O'Fallon family, Emma and McClain and Tim and Ira and Lizzie. And Mom and Daddy, too. Weren't they enough for Annie without her needing Bo?

They were! They had to be.

"Know what?" Emma said. "Know how we talked about dance lessons? Well, I've decided. I definitely do want to take Irish dancing."

"Emma," Annie said, "Irish dance is lovely. But how's that going to help with the friends problem? They're doing hip-hop!"

"I know," Emma said. "But I was thinking I could do both, maybe. And if I learned Irish dance, then I could come with you on Sunday nights. Okay? Maybe this Sunday, even?"

"Well," Annie said slowly. "We'd have to ask your mum and daddy, wouldn't we? I mean, since it's nighttime, you have homework and bathtime and all kinds of things to do Sunday nights."

"They'll change their minds and say yes," Emma

said. Although of course, she wasn't sure of that at all.

"Then maybe," Annie said. "Only not this Sunday."

"Why not this Sunday?" Emma said.

"Because we'll be getting ready for the contest. Our day to perform is Tuesday, so we have just a few days left to practice. It's a very important contest."

"Do you get a trophy?" Emma asked.

"Even better," Annie said. "The winning couple goes on to the nationals. Maybe even the internationals. Ireland, maybe."

"Couple?" Emma said. "You and Bo? *Together?*"

Annie didn't answer. She was frowning and looking around. They had walked a long way and were quite deep into the woods. It was also getting pretty dark. Annie switched on her flashlight.

"Where are you, McClain?" she called.

"Hiding," McClain answered.

Annie laughed. "Hiding where?"

"Right here!" McClain said.

"Right here, *where?*" Emma said, mean sounding. She couldn't get a single conversation finished with Annie. Annie and Bo might go away *together?*

Annie swooped the flashlight beam in a long, slow circle. And there, practically right alongside them, but way, way back in a crack in a huge boulder, was McClain.

"Come on out," Emma said.

"Yes, do come out," Annie said. "It's going to be dark any minute now."

"I can't. I'm stuck," McClain said.

"McClain!" Emma said, using her maddest voice. "You are not stuck."

McClain giggled. "I'm a little bit stuck. You'll have to pull me out."

Emma gritted her teeth. "Okay, okay!" she said. "I'm coming. I'll help you."

"Be careful now," Annie said. "Want me to do it?"

Emma shook her head. "She's not stuck. She's just being a pain." She wiggled her way into the crack in the rocks. She held out her hand, and McClain grabbed it with both her own.

Emma pulled.

McClain wasn't stuck at all. She popped out like a little cork, right up against Emma's chest. Emma lost her balance. They both tumbled backward and landed on their bottoms. Right in the middle of the muddy stream.

Chapter Ten

A Truly Brilliant Plan

Gross! Emma was soaked through, and McClain was covered in mud, and Annie was pretty splashed with mud, too. Not only that, but Emma had tripped over her bag of kindling when she fell, and it had tumbled into the stream. The dry twigs wouldn't be so dry anymore.

Annie decided there was enough firewood in her bag, anyway, and so they turned around and started back to the campsite. McClain insisted her pants were so wet she couldn't walk, so Annie carried her piggyback. Of course, that meant Emma couldn't ask again about Sunday or anything, not with McClain leaning over Annie's shoulder. Besides, how could Emma even get a word in? McClain was bubbling on about bears and chipmunks and other stuff that she swore she had seen while she was hiding.

When they arrived back at the campsite, Emma saw that Daddy and Tim and Bo had the big tent set up under some trees. Right alongside it was Bo's tiny pup tent. Emma headed straight for the big tent and her backpack to find dry pants. Annie and McClain came, too.

Once they had all changed into dry clothes, Daddy took the kindling that they had collected and in just a few minutes, he had a roaring fire going. They put their wet clothes close to the fire to dry out, and Daddy began cooking the hot dogs and hamburgers.

Everyone else hustled about, helping to get the meal ready. The whole time, Emma stuck close to Annie, careful not to let Bo get near her. She needn't have worried, though. Bo was busy with the little ones, helping to sharpen sticks for their marshmallows and hot dogs, and he never even came close to Annie. And later, when everyone settled around the fire, Ira cozied up on one side of Bo, and Lizzie curled up next to him on the other, and he put one arm around each of them.

When everyone was finished eating, and it was totally dark, Daddy began telling ghost stories. He did this every camping trip, but he didn't tell scary ghost stories because the twins were so little. His stories were more silly than scary. The first one was about an owl that was lonely and liked to sleep in tents with little kids. The owl's name was Marvin, and he hid in the trees right above them. And, Daddy said, Marvin might come flying into their tent—*this very night*. Daddy waved his hands and wiggled his fingers like a pretend, lonely owl.

Everybody giggled and made believe they were scared of the owl, but nobody was, really. Except maybe for Tim. Emma noticed that he kept looking up at the trees, then back at the fire, then up at the trees again. Emma worked her way around the campfire to be close to him. She knew Tim better than anybody, and she figured he'd feel better with her next to him. She had another reason to be close to him, too.

When the others started singing silly camp songs, Emma leaned close. "Tim?" she said softly. "Bo's scared of bears."

"So?" Tim said.

"So," Emma said.

"So what?" Tim said. "Everybody's scared of bears."

"Yeah, but this is different. Annie doesn't like guys who get scared. She said she goes for men like her dad."

"How do you know?"

"She told me. She said her daddy was her hero.

And Bo said if there was a bear around, he'd run. He wouldn't even rescue Annie! So if we saw a bear, or if we thought we saw a bear . . ."

"We won't see a bear," Tim whispered.

"We might," Emma whispered back.

"Bet," Tim said.

Emma sighed. "We *might* see one. I mean, it's possible."

It was definitely possible. Because Emma was coming up with a plan. At home, they had a book about a kid who went camping and pretended there were bears around. And what this kid did was, he just went outside the tent when it was dark, and he leaned against it hard. Everybody inside thought it was a bear because he made grunting and growling noises and the tent was bulging inward as though a huge bear was pushing against it. Emma could do that, too. And since Bo was in his own tent, she wouldn't have to scare everyone in her tent, just lean against Bo's tent and . . .

She picked up a stick and began scratching around in the dirt, thinking more. *And then . . .* and then she'd growl or stomp or something and he'd wake up and come running, or screaming.

"Emma?" Tim said softly. "They'll notice you're not in the tent. They'll see that you're missing. And they'll know it's you out there."

Mind reader! Had he read the same book?

She scrunched up her face, but she didn't turn to him. She just shrugged. "I wouldn't do anything like that," she muttered.

"Emma? Tim?" Daddy said. "What are you two cooking up? Do you have a story for us?"

"Uh, we're working on it," Emma said. "It's a . . . a soccer story."

"I have a story!" McClain piped up. "Want to hear it?"

"Surely do!" Annie said. "Come sit on my lap and tell us." She patted her lap, and McClain scooted over.

"Okay," McClain said. "Ready? Once upon a time there was a cat that couldn't meow."

"Why not?" Ira said.

"I don't know," McClain said. "She just couldn't. So first, she asked the wise owl to help her. He said, 'take a deep breath, blow it out, and meow.' But nothing happened."

"Was it the same owl? The one who was lonely?" Ira asked.

"No!" McClain said. "So next she asked the smallest ant. He said—"

"Ants can't talk," Lizzie said.

"Will you two just hush?" Mom said. "Let McClain tell her story. Go on, McClain."

"Okay!" McClain said. "So the ant said, 'take a deep breath and blow it out and whistle at the same time.' But nothing happened. Then she asked the wise butterfly. He said to blow out some air, then breathe some in, then scream. And the cat did a meowww! And it worked. She hugged the butterfly and ran away. She still meows. The end."

"That's a great story, McClain!" Annie said. "Did you think that up all by yourself?"

"Uh, huh!" McClain said.

"Well, that's wonderful!" Daddy said, clapping his hands. Mom clapped, too.

"You do understand about cats, McClain," Bo said. "You'll make a very good vet."

Emma just rolled her eyes.

Pretty soon, Mom announced that it was bedtime. First, though, they all had to go to the spooky outdoor bathroom place. It was the only thing Emma didn't like about camping. There were spiders everywhere, and once, she had seen a bat. They did it as fast as they could, and when they were finished, they went back to the tents. Bo said good night—he didn't kiss Annie—Emma watched and then went into his tent, and the rest of the family got into the big tent. Everybody crept into their sleeping bags and zipped them up. The only one who didn't have a sleeping bag was Woof.

Emma patted the bottom of the tent beside her and put down the blanket they had brought for him. Woof came over and settled next to her.

Her plan was this—she would stay awake. When everyone got quiet, all nice and sound asleep, she'd get up. She'd slip out of the tent and around the back of Bo's tent. She'd do all those things she had thought of before—lean in, make bear noises. Bo would wake up. He'd probably scream. He might even come running into their tent. Emma could hurry back into her own tent and say she'd gone off to the creepy bathhouse and . . . and . . . and next thing she knew, she was waking up. It was totally dark in the tent. Black dark. She had promised herself that she would stay awake! How could she have fallen asleep? She didn't know what time it was. Or what had awakened her. Had she slept a long time? Or just a little bit?

She sat up quietly, trying to keep her sleeping bag from rustling. She could hear breathing, quiet snoring, too. She peered around the tent. With the bright moonlight seeping through the canvas, she could just make out the other sleeping bags and the lumpy shapes of people inside them. Daddy— snoring. Mom. She was snoring, too, little whistling breaths. Annie. Tim. A little shape—McClain. Two even littler shapes—Ira and Lizzie.

81

And outside, a big fat shape—a shadow— looming over the back of the tent. Emma sucked in her breath. Something big. Something dark. A bear!

She put a hand to her throat. Her heart was pounding wildly. She started to reach out for Tim. But no, she shouldn't wake him up. He'd be terrified. Daddy!

She turned and looked toward the back again.

The shadow moved. And then, she heard it—a low, dark growl.

A bear. A real, true bear!

Chapter Eleven

A Bear Comes to Call

Except it wasn't. Emma opened her mouth to scream. But the scream got caught in her throat. Because she realized something. The sound. The growl. The shadow. She thought she recognized it.

She looked around her, felt for Woof and his blanket. There was a blanket. But no Woof. She squinted at the tent opening. The zipper could be opened from the top or the bottom. It was open at the bottom, about a foot. Had Daddy forgotten to zip it? Or did Woof just nose it open? He must have done it and snuck out. It was him out there.

Emma felt so relieved.

She turned and looked at the back of the tent again. The shadow moved. Woof. Just Woof. He was wagging his little stubby tail.

And there wasn't any bear with him. Woof wouldn't be wagging his tail if a bear were out there.

Emma was so glad Woof hadn't been eaten. And so glad that she had woken up. She'd go outside now, and she and Woof could pretend to be bears together. They would scare Bo, and he'd yell his head off and wake everyone up. Especially Annie. Then Annie would see that Emma was brave and Bo was just a big scaredy-cat.

Emma tried wiggling out of her sleeping bag. It was zipped too tight for her to get out without unzipping it. Carefully, she tugged at the zipper.

ZIP! It sounded like a train rattling through the tent.

She sucked in her breath. She looked around. Nobody had moved. How come zippers were so noisy at night? They weren't that noisy in the daytime. And the zipper had hardly budged in spite of all the noise it had made.

Maybe if she unzipped it slooowly. . . . Real slowly.

But even slowly was loud. Emma couldn't do it. She gave up. She got to her feet unsteadily, the bag still snug around her middle. She wiggled her hips, trying to get the bag to fall down. She did a little dance. She wriggled some more.

Outside the tent, she could hear Woof still snuffling and pawing at the ground. For just a moment, she wondered again if there might be a real bear out there. But no, she decided. Not with the way Woof was acting. His head was down, and he was pawing the ground like he was playing with a chipmunk or field mouse or something. If it were a bear, he'd be scared just as she would be and might even have run away by now.

She wiggled even harder and finally the bag fell down around her ankles. Slowly, she stepped out of it. She staggered and nearly fell but caught herself just in time.

And then, standing up like that, she realized—she was freezing! But she couldn't stop for a sweatshirt, even if she could have found one in the dark.

Silently, barely even breathing, she stepped past Tim. He didn't move. She crept past Daddy, her head turned away. For some reason, she didn't want to look at him. She had a feeling that even in his sleep he'd notice and open his eyes if he felt her looking at him.

Emma got to the tent's opening and stopped. There was no way she could unzip that big, fat zipper. It would wake up everybody, bears even, if they were out there. She'd just have to wiggle out through the space at the bottom that Woof had used.

Emma took one more look around. Nobody had

moved. Quietly, she lowered herself till she was sitting on the tent floor right in front of the opening. Then, very, very quietly, she stuck her legs through the opening till they were completely outside the tent. It was even colder out there! She was glad she had kept her socks on. She tilted backward and lay flat on the tent floor. Then, slithering and wriggling, she used her elbows to propel herself out of the tent, like a snake on its back. There! She was out. All of her was outside the tent—and freezing cold. She breathed in deeply, then she silently, carefully, scrambled to her feet.

Woof came bounding around the tent, his footsteps on the dry branches loud in the silence.

"Hush!" Emma whispered.

She grabbed his collar and pulled him close. "Stop prancing around!" she whispered.

He stopped waggling so much, but he panted at her, happy to have company.

"And don't breathe so loud!" she whispered. She led him away from the tent and over to the picnic table.

"Okay," she said, sitting down for a minute to catch her breath while still holding tight to his collar. "We have work to do. You won't tell on me, will you?"

Woof just looked at her. He wasn't like

Marmaduke who spoke to her—well, pretend-spoke to her. But she knew Woof wouldn't tell even if he could.

She put both arms around his neck, hugging him close, feeling how warm he was, then looked up at the night sky. At home, there weren't stars like this. Here, they were so bright they seemed to tangle in the branches of the trees. And there were zillions of stars, zillions and zillions of them. The full moon shone brightly, and when the tree branches moved, shadows danced.

A bird called from high in a tree and was answered by another bird, right close by. Emma smiled. She hadn't known that birds sang at night. Maybe they were children birds who couldn't sleep. Like her. And then, as she looked around at everything so beautiful and still and peaceful, she got a funny feeling inside. It felt a little bit sad, not crying sad though, but beautiful sad. She had never felt like this before.

She sat for a few moments, wondering about it, shivering in the cold. And then Woof strained against her, like he was saying, *Let's go!*

"Okay," she whispered, but she sat for just one more minute, feeling the silence, before she stood up. "I'm ready," she whispered. "Let's go. We're going to be a great bear."

Emma held tight to Woof's collar, keeping him close to her side. Together, they made a huge, wide circle around both tents, Emma stepping carefully, trying not to make a sound, and Woof galumphing like an elephant. She kept telling him to shush, even though she realized it wasn't his fault that he didn't know how to tiptoe.

When they got to the back of the tent, Emma paused, peering into the dark. It was hard to see, even with the moon shining brightly, because Daddy had set up both tents under the trees. Emma stood silently, waiting for her eyes to adjust to the darkness, holding her breath, wishing that Woof could breathe more quietly. Woof began tugging on his leash.

"In a minute," she whispered.

And then she had a bad thought: what if Woof started barking? She bent toward him. She put her whole hand around his snout, holding his mouth closed, like she had been taught to do when she and Daddy took Woof to dog training school.

"Hush!" she whispered. "No barking. No. Barking."

Woof snuffled through his closed mouth, and he seemed to nod. Emma let go of his snout.

"Good dog," she said. She got a tighter grip on his collar and then carefully tugged him forward.

Except Woof wouldn't go forward. He stood firm. He braced his legs.

"Come on!" Emma whispered, tugging harder. "Come!"

But Woof wouldn't come. A deep, dark growl came from his throat.

"Stop it!" she whispered.

Woof growled again, more menacing this time, low down in his throat. Emma could feel the fur on his neck raise up under her hand.

"What's the matter?" she whispered. Her heart began racing again, and she swallowed hard.

Woof strained against her hand, growling even louder, his whole body seeming to rumble. He was looking toward some low hanging branches right alongside them.

Emma turned—and saw it—saw what he must be seeing. A shadow, dark and close to the ground, crouched under a low branch. A bear! Was it? No. Maybe. Not a big one. A little one. But even little bears could—

And then Woof lunged forward. Hard. He yanked himself free of Emma's hand. He pulled so hard, so fast, that Emma tumbled forward onto the ground. She landed on all fours.

Woof flung himself at the little bear. And stopped. He yelped. He howled. He put a paw up and swiped at his own face.

Emma began to choke. She coughed madly. She tried to cover her eyes. They stung. They stung like crazy. Tears ran down her face.

Woof began running in circles. Yelping. Crying. Barking hoarsely.

Everything stunk! Emma stunk. Woof stunk. The whole world was stinking, smelling, stinking stunk.

Not a bear.

Worse than a bear.

A skunk.

They had been sprayed by a skunk.

Chapter Twelve
Everything Stinks

Everybody woke up. The little kids howled. Tim and Daddy and Bo raced out of the tents and rushed Woof off to the stream to wash him and rinse his eyes. Mom hustled everyone outside, away from the tent and over to the picnic table. That wasn't far enough, though. The smell followed them. Thank goodness there weren't many other campers in the campground, because they all had to go to the next site and then the next one, before they were finally far enough away. They could still smell skunk, but at least they could breathe.

Annie had grabbed towels and soap and clothes and now hurried Emma off to the bathhouse. Before they had gone down the path, Annie said something to Mom about getting tomato juice because that took the smell away, but Mom said they hadn't brought any along. In the bathhouse,

Emma got into the shower. She stood under the water and ran it and ran it and ran it till there was no more hot water. Even after washing again and again with shampoo and soap, she was still kind of stinky. And her hands and knees were all scraped up where she had fallen when Woof took off after the skunk. And, of course, she had the other scrape on her arm, and the soap and water made it all sting. But by the time the hot water was gone, she didn't smell quite as bad as she had before.

After Emma got dried off and had put on clean clothes, she and Annie walked back up the path to the campsite. Annie took Emma's hand.

"Are you okay?" Annie asked. "You must have been scared."

"I'm okay," Emma said. "Just mad. Stupid skunk! Do you think Mom and Daddy are mad?"

Annie laughed. "Probably a little bit. What were you doing out there, anyway?"

Emma shrugged. She didn't answer. She'd have to have an answer for Mom and Daddy, though. She knew that. She'd already planned what to tell them—that she woke up because she had to go to the bathroom, and then she saw that Woof was missing. She hadn't wanted him to run away, so she'd gone out to get him. She didn't think she'd say anything about a bear because she had a feeling that they'd get even madder than they were now.

Annie didn't seem to be waiting for an answer. She only laughed and pulled Emma close. "I know," she said. "It's hard to sleep sometimes. Especially when you're not in your own bed."

If you only knew! Emma thought.

It was almost morning. The sky was just beginning to lighten when they got back to the campsite. Mom had gotten the little ones dressed, bundled up in their sweatshirts and stuff, and they were huddled around her at the picnic table. Daddy had a big fire going in the pit nearby, and he was making coffee and bacon. Emma could smell it. Lots better than skunk. Tim and Bo were down by the stream with Woof. Even from so far away, Emma could tell that Woof was still awfully smelly. He was also bedraggled and wet and forlorn looking. Tim was rubbing him dry with a towel, and Bo was talking to him, rubbing his neck and ears. Both Tim and Bo waved to them.

Emma sat down at the table, just as Daddy handed Mom a mug of coffee. That was good. Mom was always a little grouchy in the mornings before she had her coffee. Mom gently moved the little ones off her lap and wrapped both hands around the coffee mug. The little kids scrambled over to Annie and climbed into her lap instead.

"You made a skunk come!" McClain said, glaring at Emma from the circle of Annie's arms.

"I didn't *make* him come!" Emma said. "He came all on his own."

"Did you bother him?" Ira said.

"Like kick him or anything?" Lizzie asked.

"I didn't *bother* him! Or kick him," Emma said. "He bothered me!"

Daddy turned away from his cooking and put a hand on Emma's hair still wet from the shower. "How are you doing, sweetie?" he asked. "Do you feel better?"

Emma nodded.

"Still pretty smelly, though," Daddy said, wrinkling up his nose. But he was smiling. Emma was surprised. He didn't seem mad—at least, not much.

Except then he added, "So? Can you tell your mother and me what you were doing out there in the dark? You and Woof?"

Emma stared down at her scraped-up hands. She hated lying. And it seemed as though that's all she'd been doing lately. She really wanted to tell them what she was feeling—about Bo and how worried she was that he would take Annie away and that she had invented the plan about a bear so Annie would see that Bo wasn't so great, not a hero or anything, that he was actually a big scaredy-cat since he wouldn't even rescue her. And all those things. But she couldn't. She just couldn't. She sighed.

"It's just that I woke up and Woof was gone," she said.

That was true.

"And I was scared that he'd run away."

That was partly true.

"Because he didn't have his leash on."

That was true.

"So I went out to get him."

That was true, too. Sort of.

"But when I got outside, I didn't know there was a skunk in the bushes."

That was really true.

"Well, I would guess not," Daddy said. "But maybe instead of going out there alone, you could have woke me up? Or Mom?"

Emma shrugged. "But then you guys would have gotten sprayed instead. Besides, you were both snoring."

"So?" Mom said.

"So I thought it might take too long for you to

wake up. And by then Woof would be gone."

"Woof doesn't often run off," Daddy said. "You know that."

Emma shrugged. "I know," she said. She leaned her elbows on the table and propped her chin in her hands. Suddenly, she realized how tired she was. She'd been awake half the night, and the sun wasn't even up yet. The birds were only just beginning to wake up, chirping sleepily in the tree tops. Emma wondered if any of them were the same ones who'd been up with her in the night. She wondered if they were as tired as she was.

She looked at the little kids who were half asleep in Annie's lap. Annie was rocking all three of them, back and forth, back and forth. Emma kind of wished she could be rocked like that. She felt a little sad and even lonely.

And then, as she watched, she saw Bo coming toward them from the stream. He came over to the picnic table and stood beside Annie. He laid one hand gently on Annie's hair and smiled down at the little kids.

Annie turned her face up to him. Annie wasn't really lonely now. She had Bo. She didn't even need Emma anymore.

Emma straightened up. She took a deep breath. Before she could even think of "consequences," she said, "See, I couldn't wait for you to wake up because I thought there was a bear out there."

"You *what?*" Daddy said. "You thought there was a *bear?* What made you think that?"

Emma looked at Bo. "There was like . . . growling."

"Wait a minute," Daddy said. He set down the frying pan he'd been using, turned to Emma, and leaned down so his face was right level with hers. "You thought there was a bear and so you went out? To check?"

"Not to check. To save Woof." Again, Emma looked at Bo.

"Did you want to get mauled? Killed?" Mom gasped.

McClain's head popped up. "There was a bear!" she cried.

And, of course, that started the twins howling.

"Oh, come, come, come," Annie crooned. "Don't fuss. Emma only *thought* that. There are no bears. Really."

"But I did hear something, Annie!" Emma said. "And Bo, you should go look behind your tent. Just in case."

Annie stood up. "Now, come, come!" she said to the little ones. "Let's not fuss. Let's go see how that big old dog of yours is doing. Away with you!"

And she ushered them in front of her.

Bo stood for a moment, frowning at Emma, and then he nodded a few times. "I'll go check around the tent," he said quietly.

And all of them headed off.

When they were gone, Mom said, "Emma, did you *really* think there was a bear out there?"

Emma nodded. "I did. I thought so. I didn't see one. But I heard growling."

Daddy shook his head. "But you didn't actually *see* a bear," he said. "The growling you heard came from Woof. We would have known if there was a bear. We'd all have heard him. Bears are big. They make huge noises. They crash around. They don't tiptoe. Besides, Woof would have made a terrible racket."

"He did make a terrible racket!" Emma said.

"He made a racket about a *skunk!*" Daddy said.

"Maybe," Emma said. "But I think there *was* a bear."

"Emma," Daddy said. "Now tell me something. What were you planning to do if there *was* a bear out there?"

What would she have done? Probably run screaming. But she knew what to say. "Nothing!" she said. "I wouldn't have to because the bear would run away. Remember what you told us? You said bears are more scared of us than we are of them."

She knew that was so totally untrue. She'd have been terrified.

Daddy looked at Mom. Mom looked at Daddy. Mom buried her face in her hands. Daddy closed his eyes and shook his head.

Neither of them said anything more for a few minutes, a long few minutes. Emma wondered what they were thinking. She wondered how mad they were. She wondered how much trouble she was in. She wondered if her bear story had made any difference to Annie and Bo at all.

Finally, Mom took her hands away from her face. "Emma," she said very, very quietly, "it's a good thing for you that the travel part of soccer is over. I am not letting you out of my sight for a while. Except for school."

And dance, Emma said.

But she only said that inside her head.

She'd just have to wait a few more days. Till things got back to normal.

Chapter Thirteen
Best Friends Again

The rest of the weekend was stinky, and not just because of the smell. They couldn't spend Saturday and Sunday at the campsite like they had planned. The little kids were tired and crabby. McClain kept crying and thinking she saw bears behind every tree. Once, she screamed and pointed at a big shape by the tent. The twins burst out crying. Daddy went to look. It was a rock.

But the real reason they had to come home was that everything stunk. The tent, their clothing, their sleeping bags, everything—they all stunk. Even the food tasted like skunk. And Woof stunk the worst of all.

So they packed up and went home. On the way, they dropped Woof off at the vet so Dr. Pete could get him de-smelled. Dr. Pete gave them some stuff for Emma to wash with, too. And once they got home, Mom and Daddy spent most of the day washing and airing everything out.

Emma thought Mom and Daddy sent her lots of annoyed looks while they were doing all that. But even worse, Annie disappeared with Bo somewhere.

Sunday didn't get any better. Annie stayed up in her apartment and didn't come down all day. And when Sunday night came, she went off to Irish dance. Without Emma. And with Bo. And in just two more days, she was going to be in that contest with him.

Monday morning didn't feel good, either. Emma knew Luisa was still mad at her. And she also knew that she *had* to talk to her. But would Luisa want to talk? Would she want to make up? Or would she be best friends with Katie and ignore Emma?

At school, the bell rang just as Luisa arrived, out of breath and almost late. So Emma had no chance to talk to her then. It wasn't until they were outside on the playground at recess that she was able to get near Luisa. But even then, she didn't get her alone.

Because Katie was right beside her.

Emma grabbed Luisa's coat sleeve. "Luisa!" she said. "I need to talk to you."

Katie stepped between Luisa and Emma. "You can't," Katie said.

"I wasn't talking to *you*," Emma said.

"And Luisa's not talking to *you!*" Katie said. "Are you, Luisa?"

Luisa stared at the ground. She didn't look at Katie. She didn't look at Emma. She just shook her head.

"Luisa!" Emma said. "Stop it. What's the matter?"

"You know what's the matter," Katie said.

"Luisa can *talk*, you know!" Emma said, glaring at Katie. She turned back to Luisa. "Luisa?" she said.

Luisa raised her head. She sent a mean look to Katie and an even meaner look to Emma. "What?" Luisa said—and she made her voice all mean, too.

"Don't talk to her, Luisa!" Katie said. "You said you weren't going to."

"I'm not *talking!*" Luisa said. "I'm just listening. For a minute!" She turned back to Emma. "What?" she said again. It didn't sound quite so mean this time.

"Can I talk to you, just you?" Emma asked. "Without Katie?"

"No," Katie said.

"Will you shush up?" Emma said, swinging around to face Katie. "Do you think you control Luisa or something?"

Emma turned back to Luisa. She saw something

—were there tears in Luisa's eyes? But Luisa had dipped her head down again, and Emma couldn't see her face clearly. But yes—Luisa's breath sounded trembly. Like Emma's did when she was about to cry.

Why? It made Emma feel terrible. She hadn't meant to make Luisa cry! And then, Emma thought she knew what was happening. She knew it because it was the same thing that had happened Thursday when she and Luisa and Katie had first talked about the talent show.

The problem was sharing. Katie had become Luisa's friend. And Emma was Luisa's friend, too—at least, she hoped she still was, if Luisa ever got over being mad at her. Emma and Luisa had been friends forever. Before Katie even moved here. But now Luisa had two friends. And those two weren't friends with each other. They didn't even like each other and that made Luisa feel bad. And weird. And trapped. Or something. Maybe caught in the middle.

Luisa wanted both friends.

Emma hated that. And for some reason, it reminded Emma of the walk in the woods the other night with Annie and how she had to share Annie with McClain. And the whole sharing thing made her all confused feeling. Still, she knew what she had to do, and she took a deep breath. "Luisa?" she said. "I didn't mean to read your journal. Well, I did mean to. But I shouldn't have."

"Then how come you did?" Luisa said. "I thought you were my friend."

"I am," Emma said. "I am your friend." And then she said it, said just what she had been thinking. And she said it with Katie there, too. "See, I was afraid you'd change your mind. I thought you'd want to dance with Katie. Instead of doing jump rope with me."

"But I *told* you I'd do jump rope, didn't I?" Luisa said.

Emma nodded. "I know," she said. "I know. But I was worried and that's why I tried to peek at your journal even though I know I shouldn't have. It's just because I thought that . . ." She swallowed hard. "I thought that hip-hop dance is way more fun and way cooler than jump rope, and I still think it is, and I was scared you'd think so, too."

"Well, we do think so," Katie said.

Emma just sent Katie a look.

"And you know what else?" Luisa said, ignoring Katie and looking right at Emma. "I told Katie I wouldn't do dance with her. Because I had already promised you. Even if dance is cooler. Didn't I, Katie?"

104

Katie nodded. And for once, she didn't speak.

Emma sighed. "I'm sorry," she said. She stared down at her feet. She wasn't sure what to say next. Should she say, "Sure, go ahead, it's all right if you dance with Katie?" But she couldn't! She wanted to do something in the show with Luisa. Luisa was her best friend. It was all so messed up.

All three of them were silent—even Katie who usually never shut up. Luisa had pulled a strand of hair into her mouth and was sucking on it intently.

After a minute, Luisa spit out her hair and tossed her head. "I have an idea," she said.

"What?" Emma said.

"You can dance with Katie *and* me," Luisa said. "The three of us can dance together."

"No way!" Katie said.

"Yes, way!" Luisa said, turning to Katie. "If I dance with you, Emma has to dance, too."

"But she doesn't know how!" Katie said. "She'll spoil it."

"No she won't," Luisa said. "She can learn." She looked at Emma. "Can't you?"

Emma was so surprised, she could hardly even speak. All three of them dance together? So much better than jump rope. All the kids in class would be so impressed. Everybody loved hip-hop. But did Emma really want to perform with Katie?

Anyway, Emma remembered something then and shook her head. "Can't," she said.

"Yes, you can!" Luisa said. "It's not that hard."

"It's not that," Emma said. "See, I didn't tell you yet, but I got in a lot of trouble over the weekend. Mom and Daddy won't let me take dance lessons. They said they weren't even letting me out of their sight."

"Then don't take lessons. We can teach you!" Luisa said. She turned to Katie. "Can't we, Katie?"

Katie folded her arms. "No!" she said. "I mean, yes, we can teach her. But she can't learn that fast! She'll mess up and wreck our whole performance."

"Oh, stop it, Katie!" Luisa said. "Don't be mean."

Luisa looked at Emma. "There's a lot of fancy stuff, like kicks and stuff. And spinning on the floor. But you can learn it quick."

"Okay! I have an idea," Katie said. "We could teach her background or something. She could probably learn that."

Right. Background. Or something, Emma thought.

And then suddenly, Luisa did a little dance step, bumping up against Emma's hip, then spinning away toward Katie.

Katie did a little dance step, too, spinning around so she and Luisa were back to back, spinning again so they were face to face. Then they both did this big kick out, like a karate kick.

It reminded Emma of a TV show she had seen. There were some guitar players and behind them were some background dancers doing high kicks. One of the dancers had a parrot on his shoulder and the other had an iguana. Emma had liked the iguana. She wondered if Mom would let her get one for the show.

She thought about Marmaduke. Maybe she could use Marmaduke in the dance!

"See?" Luisa said, stopping in front of Emma, breathing fast. "It's not that hard."

Emma nodded. Luisa was right. It didn't look that hard. Not the dancing part, anyway. But the other part—sharing a friend, a best friend? That was hard.

That was really, really hard.

And it made Emma think of Annie. And Bo. She sighed. It was so complicated. But she'd figure it all out. Somehow. At any rate, she'd share Luisa, and all three of them would dance together, she and Luisa and Katie. And they'd have fun, too.

Who knows, she thought? *Maybe she'd even end up being friends with Katie.*

But then she shook her head.

Nah. Probably not.

Chapter Fourteen
Annie's Big Day

It was Tuesday morning. The day Annie was going to her dance contest. With Bo.

Emma was up early, before anyone. Almost always, she was first one up, but this morning, she was up super early. She just hadn't been able to sleep. If Annie and Bo won, they'd go to the national and then maybe the international contests. Maybe even to Ireland. And they'd do more and more stuff together.

Emma was worried. And mad. She knew she should share Annie. Just like she was sharing Luisa with Katie. But she didn't have to like it.

She got dressed, let Marmaduke and Marshmallow out to play, and then went downstairs. First, though, she remembered to close her door tightly behind her.

The whole house was still asleep, all but Woof.

He came galloping down the stairs after her. In the kitchen, Emma got Woof's electronic collar and put it on him and opened the back door so he could run free. Daddy had one of those invisible fences installed so Woof couldn't run away. After Emma let him out, she put food in his food dish and water in his water bowl.

Then, she set out food and water for Kelley, setting her bowls on top of the dryer in the laundry room. They were kept there because if Kelley's food was on the floor, Woof always ate it up.

Emma looked around for what else she could do. She wasn't trying to be especially good or helpful or anything. She just felt like she had to do something.

She looked at the clock. Annie had said she'd have breakfast with them before she left for dance. Still, Annie didn't usually come down till about eight. It wasn't even seven o'clock yet.

Maybe Emma should set the table for breakfast. Why not?

She got out the dishes and place mats. She folded up some paper napkins. She carried them all to the dining room. Then she came back to the kitchen for the juice glasses. She saw the coffee pot on the counter. Maybe she could make coffee for Mom. Mom would be surprised. And happy. But no. Emma didn't know how to make coffee, and she'd probably just mess it up.

She went to the back door again and saw Woof running around outside. She was just about to let him in when the phone rang in the kitchen.

Emma hurried to the counter and picked it up. "Hello?"

For a moment, there was silence on the other end. And then a voice said, "Emma? Emma, is that you?"

Yuck. Bo. "Yes," Emma said. "It's me."

"I'm sorry to call so early," Bo said. "But is Annie there? She doesn't answer her cell phone."

"She's probably lost it," Emma said. "Again. She's always losing it."

"Well, will you give her a message?" Bo asked. "I mean, she's not downstairs yet, is she?"

"No. But I'll give her a message."

"Okay," Bo said. "It's very, very, very important. Will you tell her that our dance time has been changed? We go on at eleven o'clock. An hour earlier. Eleven o'clock. Can you remember that?"

"'Course I can remember it!" Emma said, annoyed. Did he think she was a moron? Or a little kid?

Bo laughed. "I'm sorry. Of course you'll remember. But I can't call back for a while so I'm counting on you. How's Woof? Is he still smelly?"

"He's fine," Emma said.

"That's good," Bo said. "See you soon. And you'll tell Annie. Right? Eleven o'clock. Not twelve."

You already told me that! Emma said. But she just said it inside her head. "I'll tell her," she said out loud. And she hung up.

Annie had to be at the dance hall at eleven o'clock. Not twelve.

But . . . what if . . . what if Annie didn't get there till twelve?

Emma stood by the phone, her thoughts racing around like little mice inside her head. If she didn't tell, Annie would miss her dance time. If Annie missed her dance time, she couldn't win. If Annie didn't win, she wouldn't go to the nationals. She wouldn't go anywhere. With Bo.

Emma blinked hard, surprised at herself. Of course she would tell! She would absolutely, positively tell. She would give Annie Bo's message. The minute Annie came downstairs. Really. How could she have even *thought* of doing something so horrible?

Emma could hear the little kids upstairs. They were awake and running up and down the hall. It sounded as if they were chasing each other. A door slammed and then another door. The kids were squeaking and giggling.

Emma went back into the dining room. She stood looking out the window, watching Woof cavorting around the backyard. As soon as Annie came downstairs, Emma would give her Bo's message.

After a few minutes, everyone came downstairs and into the dining room. Mom and Daddy came first, with the little kids trailing behind, tumbling around like little monkeys. McClain had Kelley tucked under her arm, as if she were a stuffed cat. Lizzie was hanging onto Daddy's leg, so that with every step Daddy took, Lizzie bumped along behind him. Lizzie was giggling, and Daddy was pretending to shake her off. And then came Annie, earlier than usual, probably because of the contest. The only family member missing was Tim. Emma knew that he liked to work on his computer before breakfast.

"Emma!" Ira said. "Me and Lizzie was looking for you!"

"I was, too!" McClain said. She dumped Kelley onto the floor, then launched herself at Emma, her arms up.

Emma bent and scooped McCain high into her arms.

"Did I hear the phone ring before?" Daddy asked.

Emma didn't answer. She just hugged McClain to her.

"Emma!" Mom said, looking around. "Did you do this? Did you set the table?"

Emma nodded.

"Good girl!" Mom said. "Thank you."

"And Woof?" Daddy said. "He wasn't upstairs in the hall. Where is he? Did you let him out?"

Emma nodded again. "Yup. And I put his collar on, too," she said.

"What a good kid you are," Daddy said.

"Isn't she," Annie said, smiling at Emma. "She's the best!"

"She's the *beast!*" McClain said. She plopped a big kiss on Emma's cheek. "Now put me down!" she said. And then she added, "Right side up!" because Emma sometimes put her on the floor upside down.

Emma set her down properly, feet first.

Mom headed out of the room for the kitchen. "Are you excited, Annie?" she called over her shoulder.

"Nervous more than anything," Annie said. But she didn't look nervous. She just looked very, very happy. She sat down at the table and lifted the twins into her lap. Ira put his little hand on Annie's

113

face. Annie nibbled on his fingers. He squealed. Then Lizzie stuck her fingers in Annie's mouth.

Emma watched them. The little kids looked so sweet and funny in their jammies with the feet. She wished she could be a little kid again. Little kids had no worries. None at all. No decisions, either. No rights and wrongs. No bad stuff. She sighed.

"Annie?" she said.

Bo called.

But she didn't say that. She would in a minute. Instead, she said, "What time will you be home tonight?"

"Probably late," Annie said. She smiled at Emma. "But I'm not leaving for a while yet. We don't perform till twelve o'clock. Plenty of time to have breakfast with you. Come sit by me."

She patted the chair next to her.

But Emma didn't go sit beside her. She just sucked in her breath.

You don't go on at twelve o'clock. You dance at eleven o'clock. Bo called.

She had to tell Annie that. She had to. And she would.

In just a minute.

Chapter Fifteen
Emma Ruins It

When Emma got home from school that day, she went directly to bed. She didn't even get undressed. She told Daddy she had a stomachache. She pulled the covers over her head. It had been the worst day of her whole entire life.

Emma had planned to tell Annie about Bo's phone call. She had meant to tell Annie. She had even *tried* to tell her.

What happened was, after breakfast, she had asked Annie to come outside with her to wait for the bus. The bus stopped right in front of their house for her and for Tim, too. So Annie said yes, and came outside. But then, when they were outside, and just when Emma was about to say, *I have to tell you something*, suddenly Annie put a hand up to her mouth.

"Oh, my goodness!" Annie cried. "Oh, my goodness. I forgot!"

"What?" Emma said.

"My tights!" Annie said. "My tights! For my costume. They're in the dryer. I have to run!" She bent and kissed Emma's forehead. "I'll talk to you tonight."

"But Annie, wait!" Emma said. "I have to tell you something."

"Honey, I can't!" Annie said. "They'll be all shrunk up!"

"Bo called!" Emma said.

But Annie had already disappeared into the house. Just as the school bus rumbled and rattled up to the curb.

And the rest of the day stunk. What was Emma supposed to do? She didn't have a cell phone. None of the kids did—at least, they weren't allowed to have them in school. So Emma hurried to the office and said she just had to call home, so the secretary said "Yes, but hurry, it's almost time for the morning bell." So Emma called Annie's cell phone, but it just rang and rang and rang and then Emma remembered—that's why Bo had called on the house phone because Annie's phone was probably lost and ringing in her pocket somewhere.

By the time Emma remembered that, the morning bell had rung, and the principal, who had been passing by, said, "Time to get to class, young lady."

"Just one more minute!" Emma said, and she dialed home. And got a busy signal.

"It's busy!" she said.

The principal was standing there, watching her. Tears had rushed up to her eyes. "I'll tell you what, Emma," he said kindly. "You go on to class. Tell me the message, and I'll call and give it to your parents in just a bit."

Like she could let that happen! Let the *principal* call? And say she had forgotten something that important? She just said "no thanks" and thought of skipping school and running back home to Annie. But she would be in such trouble.

She was stuck. Stuck with a terrible secret. She hadn't meant to ruin things for Annie. She really hadn't. But maybe it would be all right. Maybe Bo would call again. He was always calling.

But no matter how much Emma tried to tell herself it was all right, she knew it wasn't. Not only that, but she was so upset all day, she could hardly even talk to her friends, so they thought she was being mean. And Katie acted all big shot and important with Luisa.

Only one good thing happened. When the rotten school day was finally over, and the kids were on the bus going home, Jordan plopped down next to her. He didn't talk to her, just talked to Matt in the seat across the aisle. But as Emma was getting off the bus, he turned to her. "If you want," he said, "we could do something in the talent show. Together."

And then he looked away, as though he were embarrassed.

Emma thought he was about the sweetest boy in the whole world, except for Tim. And she was happy about having another friend. But even that didn't do anything to stop the ache inside of her.

Now Emma lay in bed, her arms tight around her middle, wishing she could just fall asleep. And maybe she did sleep. When she opened her eyes, it was because Mom had turned on a light in her room. Emma looked around. It was dark outside the windows. She didn't know how long she had slept.

"What's wrong, sweetie?" Mom asked, bending over and putting a hand on her forehead. "Daddy said you went right to bed. You sick?"

Emma nodded. "I don't feel good."

"You feel a little warm," Mom said. "Is it your stomach?"

Emma sighed. "Sort of. My head. Stomach. Everything."

"You might be getting the flu," Mom said. "Now sit up and let me help you get undressed and into your jammies."

Emma did, and when she was in her warm, soft pajamas, she lay back down and pulled the covers up to her chin again.

"Shall I bring you some soup?" Mom said. "Would you like that? Maybe a little chicken soup? Or tomato soup and saltine crackers? You like that."

Emma shook her head. No. She didn't want anything to eat. But she did want something—she wanted to know if Annie had left on time, if Bo had called back. But how could she ask? Then Mom would know what she had done—not done.

"Something to drink? Tea and lemon?" Mom asked. "Maybe some ginger ale?"

Emma liked ginger ale when she was sick. But even that didn't sound good. "I just want to sleep," she said.

"Okay, sweetheart," Mom said. "Go back to sleep. I'll come in later and check on you again."

And she turned off the light, went out, and closed the door.

In the dark room, Emma hugged her pillow and

cried. She had ruined everything. She had absolutely ruined everything. Annie was her best friend, her closest, nicest, funniest, best friend in the whole entire world. And Emma had done something mean to her. It didn't even matter if Annie had gotten to the dance place on time—and Emma knew that was possible. Annie *might* have left early, just in case. Or Bo *might* have called back. He hadn't said he wouldn't—only that he couldn't for a little while. Emma had comforted herself with those thoughts all day in school. But they didn't matter much. What mattered was that Emma had been mean and horrible and awful to her best friend in the whole world.

Emma thought about Margaret Ann on her soccer team who was always messing up and losing stuff and who cried about everything. But at least, Margaret Ann did some things right—she was a terrific goalie. Emma didn't think she did even one thing right.

Inside her head, Emma ran over all the ways she had messed up in the past few days—skunks and pretend bears and Katie and Luisa and reading Luisa's journal and lying about it. And not giving important messages.

She thought of getting up and bringing Marmaduke into bed to snuggle with, but even he wouldn't help her now.

She turned her head into her pillow. The pillow was all wet from crying. She flipped it over.

Her door crept open. Emma quickly swallowed back the tears and wiped her eyes. She looked at the doorway.

Ira and Lizzie were standing there, holding hands, peeking in at her. They tiptoed into her room, still hand in hand.

"We brought you a present," Lizzie whispered.

"Here!" Ira said, and he was whispering, too. "We made you a get-better card." He put it down on the bed next to her.

"Thanks," Emma said.

"You're welcome," Ira whispered.

"You're welcome," Lizzie whispered.

They turned to go, and almost bumped into McClain—and right behind McClain was Tim. And behind Tim was Daddy.

McClain had Kelley clutched tight in her arms. She didn't come in tiptoeing. And she didn't whisper, either. She bounded into the room and plopped Kelley down on Emma's bed. "Here, Emma!" she said. "You can have Kelley tonight. She'll make you better. Okay?"

"And here's my iPod," Tim said, holding it out to her. "I have lots of good music loaded onto it."

"Anything I can do?" Daddy said.

Emma looked at her brothers and sisters. She looked at Daddy. She looked at Kelley. At the iPod. At the get-better card. They were so sweet. All of them. Tim—who always thought of consequences, but never got mad at her for not thinking of consequences. She looked at McClain and Ira and Lizzie and their presents for her. And Daddy, too. And Mom, even though she wasn't here. "Thanks," she whispered. "I just want to sleep."

They all said good night and turned to go. But Daddy lingered a minute. Emma desperately wanted to ask him—*did Annie leave in time? Did Bo call back?* But she couldn't ask, just like before she couldn't ask Mom. He'd wonder why she was asking. He'd be so disappointed in her if he found out the truth.

Daddy ran a finger down her face—like he was tracing her tears. "Can I make it better?" he asked.

Emma shook her head. "No," she said. "You can't."

Weird, she thought. Weird that Daddy knew something was wrong—and not just in her stomach. But maybe not weird. He understood a lot. But he couldn't make it better. Nobody could make it better.

Right then, Emma made a decision. When Annie

got home, no matter what time, she would talk to her. She'd tell her the truth—the whole truth. She'd tell about the bear and the skunk. And Bo. And how very, very sorry she was.

And she'd say this, too: it's okay if you love Bo. It really is. I'll share you. I don't mind.

Chapter Sixteen
Emma Figures Things Out

Emma's bedroom door opened and closed a bunch of times that night. Mom and Daddy each came in to check on her again. Mom fluffed up her pillows and brought her some water and offered to read to her. But Emma said no, she just wanted to sleep.

But she couldn't sleep. Thoughts were swirling around in her head. It felt like she lay there forever waiting to hear Annie come home—to hear Bo's car. Her bedside clock said ten o'clock, and then ten thirty, and she was still wide awake and still hadn't heard Annie come home.

At eleven o'clock, her door opened, and again, Daddy came in.

"Hey, toots, still awake?" he asked. He turned on the tiny lamp on her table. He peered down at her, then put a hand on her forehead. "You don't feel too warm," he said. "You don't have a rash, do you? I've heard some kids are getting chicken pox even though they've had the vaccine."

Emma shook her head. "I don't have a rash," she said. "I just don't feel good. And I can't sleep."

Daddy frowned at her for a minute. Then he smiled. "I know what," he said. He pulled over her desk chair and placed it beside the bed. "I know how to make you fall asleep. I'll tell you one of my famous stories."

"Not a ghost story," Emma said.

"I won't tell a ghost story," Daddy said. "I'll make up an even better story. Ready?"

Emma sighed. She guessed so. It was better than staring at the clock. Or the ceiling.

"Okay," she said.

"Okay," Daddy said. "Here goes. My story is a pretend story. It's about a family full of great kids— and it's about the sweetest, smartest girl ever." Daddy paused. "Do you know who that might be?"

Emma made a face at him. "Just tell the story!" she said.

Daddy laughed. "Right. Now, the oldest in this family was a boy. He was smart, too, and sweet. He didn't get into too much mischief."

Daddy paused again.

"I know, I know," Emma said. "You're talking

about our family and you mean Tim."

"No, I don't!" Daddy said. "I just made up this story. It's about a pretend family. So in this pretend family, there was also a little sister—maybe five or so, kindergarten age. She was very independent. She loved her dolls. And her cat. She had mad tantrums. But she got over her tantrums pretty fast. She was a good kid, too. She shared her cat with her big sister."

Emma couldn't help smiling. *McClain.*

"And there were also toddlers in this family," Daddy went on. "Twins. They had learned to talk when they were really little, like just a year or so old! People were amazed. And once those twins learned to talk, they practically never stopped. Now these twins had something very special."

Emma looked up. "What?" she said.

"They had each other," Daddy said. "So they never got lonely."

"Lucky them," Emma said.

"Yes. Lucky them," Daddy said. "Now this girl I'm telling you about, her name was . . ." Daddy frowned, pretending he was trying to think up a name. "I think her name was . . . Emma?"

Emma shook her head. "No!" she said. "Emily. Remember? It's a pretend story."

"Oh, right!" Daddy said, smiling. "Emily! That's

what her name was. Now, Emily loved every single one of her brothers and sisters. They were special to her. But Emily was different. Different from everyone else in the family."

Bad, Emma said inside her head.

"Because Emma, I mean, Emily, Emily was a figure-er outer."

"A *what?*" Emma asked. "What's that?"

"A figure-er outer," Daddy said. "That means she figured things out. And that is a very, very good thing to be."

Except she figured them out all wrong, Emma said inside her head.

"Because, you see," Daddy went on. "Emily was growing up. And that's what people do when they grow up. If they see things that aren't right, they try to figure out ways to change them."

But instead she made them a whole lot worse, Emma said. But again she just said it inside her head.

"And lots of times," Daddy went on, "she did make things better. And sometimes, well, sometimes, she messed them up."

"Big time," Emma said. She said it out loud.

"But only some of the time," Daddy said.

"Like the skunk," Emma said.

Daddy nodded. "Just like the skunk," he said.

"There was no bear, you know," Emma said.

"I know that," Daddy said.

"I didn't even *think* there was a bear," Emma said.

"I figured that, too," Daddy said. "I knew you were too smart to leave the tent if a bear were out there."

"It's just because . . . I mean, I just said that so that . . . well, I knew Bo was really scared of bears."

"You don't like Bo much, do you?" Daddy said.

Emma sighed. "I like Bo okay," she said. "But I guess . . . it's just that, I don't know, just that he's so *special* to Annie."

"So are you," Daddy said.

Emma stared down at her fingers. She'd been chewing on her nails again, and they were all raggedy. "No," she said. "I'm not. I used to be, but not anymore." She sighed.

"Why not?" Daddy said.

"Because she has Bo, of course!"

Daddy laughed. "So you won't let her have *two* special people?"

Emma shrugged.

"Or five or ten even?" Daddy said. "Like that Emily I was telling you about? That wonderful girl who figures things out? She has a whole family of

128

special people. And a special, special nanny who loves her so much. And she loves the nanny back. Doesn't she?"

Emma nodded. "She does. A lot," she said. And she could feel tears welling up again.

But I want . . .

What did she want?

More. Something more. But she didn't even know what!

"Well," Daddy said, "let me think. I want to go back to my story. This Emily person I was telling you about, she has two ferrets. And she loves one way more than the other because . . ."

"Does not!" Emma said.

"Does, too," Daddy said.

"No way!" Emma said. "She loves them both. Just . . . just differently, that's all."

"Oh," Daddy said.

Emma made a face at him. Of course, he knew she didn't love one more. "Even if I had *three* ferrets, I'd love them all," she said. "Or five or ten even."

"Oh," Daddy said. "I guess I didn't know that."

Emma kept her eyes squinted up at him. "You're being silly," she said.

"I was just telling a story," Daddy said.

Still, Emma made a face at him. She figured she

knew what he was trying to say to her. But it wasn't the same, not at all. Loving two different ferrets was a lot different from sharing a nanny with . . .

It was too complicated. And for some reason, it was making Emma mad. At Daddy.

"You know what your mom and I were talking about at dinnertime?" Daddy said. "We were thinking that once you start to feel better, maybe tomorrow even, we could talk about those dance lessons you wanted."

"Really?" Emma said. "How come?"

"Just because," Daddy said. "And the traveling part of soccer is over. So maybe Irish dance? With Annie. You said you'd like Irish dance."

Emma nodded. Yes! Well, no. Well . . . maybe.

"What if I wanted to do a different kind of dance?" she asked.

"Like what?" Daddy said.

Emma shrugged. "I don't know. Maybe hip-hop. My friends are doing hip-hop."

"Really? Who?"

"Luisa. And Katie. And Luisa says there're lots of other people in her dance class."

"Hmm," Daddy said. "Katie's your friend, too, now?"

Emma shrugged. "Sort of. So can I decide and tell you tomorrow?"

"Whenever," Daddy said. "Tomorrow, or whenever you're ready." He turned out her light and bent over the bed. He pulled the covers up around her shoulders and kissed her forehead. "Anything else?" he asked softly.

Yes, did Annie get to the dance contest on time?

But even now, she couldn't ask.

"No," Emma said. "I'm okay."

"Do you think you can sleep?" Daddy asked.

"I think so," she said. "But Daddy?"

"What, sweetie?"

"Daddy, do you really think I'm good at figuring out stuff?"

"I really do," Daddy said.

"And I don't mess up too much?"

Daddy laughed. "No," he said. "You don't mess up too much. Just the right amount."

Chapter Seventeen
A (Mostly) Happy Ending

Kelley! Kelley had crept onto Emma's stomach and was turning 'round and 'round, purring like a little machine.

"Stop it, Kelley," Emma said, lifting her off. "I'm trying to sleep."

She looked at her bedside clock. Midnight. After midnight. She had fallen asleep—and Annie must be home by now! She had to be home.

Emma got out of bed. She put on her frog slippers. She opened her bedroom door. She peeked up and down the hall. The whole house was dark. Asleep. But a light was coming from under Annie's door. Annie *was* home. And awake.

Emma crept to the end of the hall. Woof was stretched out in front of Annie's door, blocking it. "Watch it, Woof," she whispered.

Woof scrambled to his feet. He stood next to

her, wagging his little stubby tail.

Slowly, quietly, Emma opened Annie's door just a crack.

No sound up there. Was Annie already asleep?

Woof nosed his head into the crack. "No, Woof!" Emma said. "Stop!"

"Emma?" Annie called softly. "Is that you?"

"Yes," Emma said. "Can I come up?"

"But of course!" Annie said.

Emma went racing up the steps, Woof bounding ahead of her. Annie was sitting on the sofa still wearing her pretty Irish dance dress. She had kicked her shoes off. She held out her arms to Emma.

Emma ran to her. And then—well, she hadn't meant for it to happen this way. She had planned exactly what she'd say and how she'd say it. She would say it very calmly. She would be very grown up. She would open her mouth and tell the truth. She wouldn't cry. And . . .

And she threw herself into Annie's arms, crying.

"Annie!" she said. "Annie, I'm sorry! I forgot to tell you Bo called. I mean, I didn't forget. I really didn't. I thought at first I wouldn't tell you because I was jealous. But I changed my mind. Honest I did. I was going to tell you—"

"Me dear, me dear!" Annie interrupted. "It's all right. It's fine!"

"It's not!" Emma said. "It was so wrong. I waited till the last minute and then . . . and then you remembered your tights shrinking up in the dryer and you ran inside and—"

"Emma, Emma!" Annie said, hugging Emma. "It's all right. It's all, all right. It is. Don't fret so."

Emma looked up. "Were you too late? Did you miss your dance time?"

"We weren't too late," Annie said. "Not at all. We didn't miss our dance time. We did just fine."

"Is Bo mad at me? For not telling you in time?"

"No!" Annie said. "I called him." She laughed. "As soon as I got me tights from the dryer. I heard you say he called just as I ran inside."

"You did? You heard me? That big noisy bus came and . . ."

Annie nodded. "I did. I heard you. And I got there in plenty of time. Too much time. I was just sitting there getting all nervous till it was time for us to go on."

Emma leaned her head against Annie. She was relieved, so, so relieved. Annie held her close, rocking her a little, back and forth, back and forth, just the way she'd held the little kids at the campground. Emma wanted to ask the next question—did you win? But at the same time, she didn't want to ask. She wasn't sure what answer she wanted to hear.

Still, she had to know, so finally, she asked. "Annie? Did you do good? Did you win?"

"We did," Annie said, stroking Emma's hair. "We did win. At least, we won today's round. We'll find out our ranking at the end of the week when it's all finished."

Emma felt her heart thud down to her toes.

We won.

We'll be spending more and more time together.

Emma couldn't even look up. She tried to say, "That's good." She really, really wanted to say it. But the words wouldn't come out.

For a long time, neither one of them said anything. Emma kept herself snuggled up against Annie, her head tucked against Annie's side. Woof had lain down in front of Emma, and Emma kicked off her slippers and buried her feet in his soft, soft fur. There was only one good thing Emma could think of—at least, she hadn't ruined everything for Annie.

"Emma?" Annie said, after a while. "You're worried about something. Is it me going away? If we win, I mean?"

Emma shook her head. "No, not that. I know that you always come back."

"What then?" Annie said.

Emma shrugged. She couldn't say it. How could she? How could she say, I'm scared you love Bo more than me? That was really, really stupid.

And then she thought of what Daddy had said about the ferrets, about loving one more than the other. And that was really, really stupid, too. She thought it was the stupidest thing she had ever heard. But she'd been thinking about it ever since Daddy had said it.

"Emma?" Annie said. "You do know how much I love you, don't you? How much I love *all* of you?"

Emma nodded. "I do," she said. She looked up at Annie. "I do," she said again. "And you know what else? It's okay if you love Bo, too. I mean it. It really is. It's even okay if you marry him. Someday."

Annie laughed. "I'm not about to marry anybody yet," she said. "Maybe someday I will. And maybe someday the good Lord will bless me with me very own family. But right now I have a whole family to take care of here."

"But you like Bo?" Emma said. "I mean, you love him, right?"

"I do," Annie said. "And I very much like spending time with him."

Emma sighed. "But you love being with us, too," she said. "Right?"

"I really, really love you," Annie said. "And I love being with you, too."

"Know what, Annie?" Emma said. "Mom and Daddy are going to let me take dance lessons."

"That's grand!" Annie said. "Just grand. What kind of dance?"

"Don't know yet," Emma said. "I haven't decided."

"Well," Annie said, "if you decide on Irish dance and want to come with me on Sunday nights, I'd love to have you. You know that."

"I do," Emma said. "I know that."

And she did know. She could go with them. Maybe even get in their way. Get in Bo's way. Get between them.

Nah. She didn't feel like doing that anymore. Besides, she hated Irish dance.

She looked down at Woof. She rubbed his back some more with her bare toes. She pressed against Annie again. She was awfully tired. Loving people was awfully tiring.

"Know what, Annie?" she said. "I think I'll do hip-hop instead."